Accolades

For *Approaching Footsteps:*

This anthology of novellas effectively combines suspense with provocative social issues. A creepy piece by Donna Hill is a standout. You'll love the bonus flash fiction pieces, which feature strong female protagonists. All in all, another winning collection from Spider Road Press.
— Pamela Fagan Hutchins, bestselling author of the USA Best Book Award-winning *What Doesn't Kill You* mystery series

Four unique voices. One distinctive collection. A compelling read from start to finish, with masterful storytelling that includes everything from history to mystery.
— Judy Penz Sheluk, Amazon International bestselling author of *Skeletons in the Attic*

These vivid, tense and startling stories will leave you breathless and longing for more. You won't want to miss this trip.
— Andrea Barbosa, author of *Massive Black Hole* and *Holes in Space*

A varied and entertaining collection that you can dip into anytime. Packed with works from different writers, the book is an altogether satisfying read. Two novellas are standouts: Rita Banerjee's *A Night with Kali* begins with a taxi ride through Kolkata during a monsoon that soon transports the reader inside a colorful story-in-a-story supernatural tale reminiscent of classic Indian literature. In *136 Auburn Lane*, novelist Donna Hill evokes a mysterious Harlem boarding house in the 1930's, where a down-and-out woman has one final chance to rescue her pitiful existence.
— Gay Yellen, author of *The Body Business* and *The Body Next Door*

For Patricia Flaherty Pagan:

The stories in Pagan's *Trail Ways Pilgrims* are masterfully told.
— R.L. Nolen, author of *Deadly Thyme*

The stories in (*Trail Ways Pilgrims*) conceal a rare literary bite. They build tension with the honest boldness that only a writer who has earned her confidence can wield, and that tension snaps to create moments and images that at are as much unexpected as they are inevitable.
— K.J. Russell, author of *The Dusty Man*

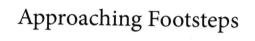

Approaching Footsteps

Approaching
Footsteps

Suspenseful Novellas
by
Rita Banerjee
Donna Hill
Jennifer Leeper
Megan Steusloff

Edited by Patricia Flaherty Pagan

Dear Gloria,

Thank you for your imagination,
and for all the lovely conversations.
Here's to great writing + stories always!

XOXO,

Rita Banerjee

Bluestockings,
NYC 3/12/17

Spider Road Press
Houston, TX
www.spiderroadpress.com

Spider Road Press gratefully thanks these generous sponsors for their support of fiction by and/or about strong women:

Sponsors

The Spitzmiller Family
Carmen P. Rinehart
Patricia E. Hanken

Nandita Banerjee
Elizabeth Lingener
Michael Pagan

Spider Road Press thanks the following donors for offering their crucial support to this collection:

Contributors

Gayle Bates
Jacqueline Burks
Eileen Brunetto
Mary Cesaratto
Carla Conrad
Stephanie Jaye Evans
Joe Flaherty
Marge Flaherty
Ryan M. Gard
Gail Goldberg
Jessica Holland
Michi Howard

Pamela F. Hutchins
Mary Ellen Johnson
Celeste M. Laak
R. M. Lagomarsino
David James Lerch
Felicia Little
Lisa Lutwyche
Eugene R. Lytton
Karen F. Marinaccio
William M. Mays
Alexander McKenzie
Mary K. McMenamin

Sarah Norwood
Julia and Al Pagan
Steven Pagan
Katherine Spitzmiller
Kim H. Sullivan
Anna J. Tonarely
Inna Vyadro
David Welling
The Wilde Collection
Ryan Workman
Gay Yellen

CONTENTS

Foreword Patricia Flaherty Pagan   11

The Reiger File Jennifer Leeper   15

A Night with Kali Rita Banerjee   41

Brave Enough to Follow Megan Steusloff   71

136 Auburn Lane Donna Hill   97

Special Reader's Bonus
Flash Fiction by the Winners and Judges
of the Spider's Web Flash Fiction Prizes

Brigida Kate Spitzmiller *First Place Winner*   127

Crazy Jen Helen Angove *Second Place Winner*   129

When I Wore Pink Boots Holly Walrath *Third Place Winner* 131

Thomas Melissa Algood *Honorable Mention*   133

Because the Sky Is Blue Andrea Barbosa *Honorable Mention* 135

Pleiku, 1969 Kate Spitzmiller *Honorable Mention*   137

Kit-Cat Clock Patricia Flaherty Pagan *2015 Judge*   141

Parcel Post Eden Royce *2016 Judge*   143

Fuzzy Dice Kathryn Kulpa *2016 Judge*   145

Contributors   149

FOREWORD

Patricia Flaherty Pagan

IF THE SOUP IS BOILING OVER, but you can't put the book down, you're reading suspense. The café is closing, the manager dims the lights, but you grip your tablet more tightly because you're reading suspense. When you wake up at five a.m. to read "just one more chapter" before getting the kids ready for school, you're reading suspense. And if you pull off the road in the rain to hear the last five minutes of an audiobook, you're listening to suspense.

Suspense can be seen as the slow-burning sister of the thriller, or the intense and eccentric cousin of the mystery. Suspense fiction builds fascination and anxiety in the reader. While reading or listening to well-crafted suspense, the audience feels compelled to find out how characters will solve an unpredictable mystery or resolve a dangerous crisis.

With this in mind, I evaluated the suspense novella submissions we received. I looked for writers offering a fresh take on peril and conflict. I always look for craft and engaging characters. I also enjoy discovering work by authors willing to accept challenges, take risks and offer unique viewpoints.

Therefore, I found myself broadening the scope of this anthology to encompass suspenseful novellas by women. Good stories don't always fit into the black leather jacket of one genre. I enjoyed the original perspectives and unexpected twists in these novellas. I hope you will, too.

Read ardently.

Patricia Flaherty Pagan
October 2016

THE REIGER FILE

Jennifer Leeper

TOM REIGER CLOSED HIS EYES and pressed his nose against the binding of *The Power and the Glory*, inhaling the bold musk created by time and paper and words perfumed in a writer's passion. He wanted to make his last few breaths in Satellite, Ohio count. Through the binding of Graham Green's masterpiece, he breathed in the library where he had worked for the past two years since he graduated from high school.

Everything about Tom Reiger looked shiny and new, as if he had just been born, from his shiny tasseled loafers to his brown eyes and wavy hair. For the last time, Tom locked the doors of the Satellite Library. He pocketed the brass key as a memento of the expiring ritual. Before the next sunset, he would be in New York City. A man with the name of an animal, 'Fox' Abel Manus, waited for him. Fox, a veteran private investigator, was going to teach Tom to become a predator of information about others.

The train from Cincinnati to New York left at 10 p.m. Tom arrived at 2 p.m. the following afternoon at Penn Station which had a grandeur more like a cathedral than any train station Tom had ever seen in Ohio. The believers swarmed him innumerably as he passed through them to the even more bustling streets of Manhattan.

"Excuse me sir—sir?" Tom grabbed at an older man passing by with his eyes. "Do you know how I can get to Ninth and Forty-First in Midtown?" Tom asked.

"Yoos gotta take the train! Ovuh there!" The old man wore a tweed jacket over long shirtsleeves and a navy sweater vest despite the heat of late June slicking down his few wisps of white hair. He animated his directions with a shaky, but emphatic index finger aimed at a dingy looking set of stairs leading into the ground across the street.

Tom was swallowed in the deep mouth of the subway. He reappeared above ground several blocks from his destination.

He started walking, unbelieving of the immensity of sights and sounds around him. Men, women and children were wrapped in colors he knew existed, but he had never seen displayed as fashion. Exotic aromas wafted from restaurants, bloating Tom's narrow spectrum of smell. Strange names on marquees, like *Cuckoo Bird* and *The Stingray*, acquainted Tom with his new world. Within the half hour, he arrived at a ten-story, brick building pinched between a neglected, boarded-up Catholic church and a movie theater showing *The French Connection*, *Straw Dogs* and *A Clockwork Orange*.

Tom entered the abbreviated foyer, where a gold-colored metal wall panel listed names linked to offices and apartments. Numbers 405 and 505 belonged to Abel Manus. Tom pressed a black plastic button.

"Hello, Mr. Manus? It's Tom Reiger."

"Eh? What's that?" A thickly accented voice spoke.

"Tom Reiger, from Ohio."

"Reiger?"

"I'm the friend of Hal Dozier's friend," Tom persisted.

There was silence.

"Ah, Dozier—right. Come on up."

A clear glass door leading away from the foyer clicked, releasing its mechanical breath so Tom could pass through. The elevator was out of order according to a piece of cardboard taped to its badly scarred doors. Tom found the stairwell which stank of body odor and urine. Old, faded blue carpeting guarded the stench all the way to Fox's office door. Fox answered on the third knock.

A man with an unevenly patched beard of grey and white on his chin, cheeks and neck and bloodshot, green eyes peered through a gap measured by the length of a chain lock. His hair must have been gray and white like his beard, but he'd shaved it to a fine dusting on his head. "Reiger?"

"Yessir." Tom smiled at the mention of his name. His teeth flashed perfectly white and straight from years of braces.

The chained gap disappeared and the door opened to present a man not so tall or wide, but somewhere in between. Except for the shaved head, he looked disheveled. A wrinkled, navy blue sports jacket with a hole in the left elbow hung askew on the man's frame over an even more wrinkled white dress shirt, open at the neck, no tie, and navy slacks. He wore one black and one white sock. Something about this ensemble hinted of a vaudevillian tramp.

"Call me Fox." Fox spoke cordially enough, but Tom couldn't help but notice a distracted look in the older man's green eyes and hands that trembled continuously.

"Nice to meet you, Fox." Tom thrust his hand into Fox's without hesitation. This forthrightness was almost starched juxtaposed with Fox's world-weary expression.

"Come in." Fox attempted to sound cheerful, though his voice and face wore cheer as comfortably as a condemned man wears his noose.

Fox's office was dark even against the backdrop of a summer's midday. Every piece of furniture was the color of midnight and seemed to cast shadows on shadows as the walls were covered in a wood paneling and ancient glass torch lamps housing dead bulbs. Out of the shadows appeared a couple of old metal desks and a brown leather couch with cushions conformed to its owner's buttocks.

Wood floors the color of charred toast complemented the overall maudlin theme. What little light leaked in through thick muslin curtains covering the room's two windows was mostly captured by a glass bouquet of liquor bottles glinting from a plastic wastebasket stationed near one of the windows.

"Sorry it's so dark. I sleep during the day. I do a lot of my rounds at night." Fox moved to switch on the row of torch lamps, which flickered and buzzed, coughing out light sickly at first.

"Rounds?" Tom asked, still clutching his suitcase.

"Rounds," Fox echoed. "You'll do rounds. Sometimes in the light. Mostly after dark. You'll watch and listen and sometimes you'll smell if you have to. You'll use every sense. You'll be more animal than human at times."

The idea of being like an animal excited Tom.

Tom's eyes widened. "What do you see on the rounds?"

"Everything."

The word thudded against Tom's brain.

"It's too much for me. I can't keep up with all the cases. That's where you come in. I need you to be able to get up to speed quickly and take over a couple of cases."

"I can do that." Tom straightened up.

Fox managed a sincere smile. "Kid, I appreciate your enthusiasm. You can sleep here, and you won't go hungry, I promise." Fox pointed to the drab couch with its owner's indention in the leather. "After you're trained up, we'll talk a salary."

"The bathroom is down the hall there." Fox pointed to a hall that hadn't existed until the torch lamps revealed it, as if the apartment were a series of primitive caves. "Tonight, you'll start your training. You might want to get a nap in. It's gonna be a long night." A heavy Bronx accent magnified Fox's sand-papery voice. "I'll get you a pillow and blanket."

"Thank you, sir."

"Just Fox. No need for titles here."

Tom nodded, accepting a pillow and a fraying wool blanket from his host. A glimmer of admiration grew for the older man in Tom's eyes.

The electric torch lamps went dark again as Tom shut his eyes and shifted against the rubbery leather of the couch to get comfortable. The leather smelled of cigarettes. He could hear the front door of Fox's office close and Fox tramping off down the hall toward the stairs leading to his apartment.

When Tom opened his eyes again, he wasn't sure what time it was because of the acute darkness.

"Hope you slept." The unmistakable diction cut through the darkness.

"I did." Tom yawned his words. It felt odd waking up in a house other than his parents', and hearing a voice other than his mother's express concern about whether he had slept.

Fox looked as if he had slept, too, but without ceremony, as his clothing hung thoroughly wrinkled and the reek of alcohol was even bolder.

"There's a shower down the hall. I'll meet you in front of the building in a half hour."

Fox handed Tom a stiff, threadbare washcloth. Tom thought of the soft, thick towels that smelled of detergent always piled in plastic baskets in his parents' bedroom.

"Thank you, si-." Tom caught himself and stopped. "Um, could I call my folks? I just want to let them know I got in okay."

"Sure, Kid. Phone's by the window."

Tom showered, and shaved with the brassy, metal razor his father gave him on his fifteenth birthday. It felt like the relic of an old life. Tom called his parents, who were eating their usual Saturday night dinner of meatloaf and mashed potatoes. Tom already missed that meatloaf. His parents already missed him.

He could hear it in his mother's voice. He promised to be home for Labor Day weekend, or sooner, if he could get away.

By the time Tom met Fox on the stoop, night blanketed the city. The mature spring air was warm, but lightly so. On this air, Tom's thoughts floated to contentment before becoming engorged again on the smells and sounds of the city. The theater crowd next door crackled with euphoric energy. Young couples in fashions Tom had only seen in the movies clung to one another, happily isolated in their lust. A few older patrons were dressed in moth-averse hats and coats. Fox waited with a couple of hot dogs wrapped in thin, translucent paper and cold sodas.

"Try one of these."

Tom thanked Fox and devoured the dog, narrowly avoiding consuming the paper along with the meat. He swallowed the soda in a few big gulps. "Good." Tom said, burping his satisfaction.

"I think the word is 'perfect,' but it's your first New York dog, so 'good' works for now. Here's my car. Let's go."

Fox drove an old red and white station wagon with one wiper broken and the other clamping a smothering of yellowed, unacknowledged parking tickets. A silvery collar of duct tape held the driver's side mirror in place.

"It gets me where I need to go," Fox said, but Tom couldn't tell whether he was trying to convince himself or his new passenger.

"My parents have one that's brown," Tom regretted the inane remark as soon as it slipped out. Hearing his thoughts aloud against the backdrop of neon sophistication, he felt very childish. Thankfully, Fox didn't seem to hear Tom's comment.

"Ever been out of Cleveland?" Fox asked as he started up the motor.

"You mean Satellite?" Tom's brown eyes looked perplexed.

"Yeah, Kid, that's what I meant."

The wagon immediately became tangled in the weekend foot and car traffic of Midtown. Though Fox appeared heavily inebriated, it seemed to be a natural state, as he maneuvered fluidly in the traffic. Tom noticed the way the cars and people moved in a choreographed dance, as everyone seemed to be cued to move at just the right moment to make room for another person or car or bicycle. At intervals, a horn or a shouted obscenity jarred this precision.

Fox punched his horn, shouting his own brand of obscenity out his window, prodding a cab to move.

Tom wasn't used to such aggressive human interaction. He came from a town and culture of quiet deliberation and even temperaments. The streets of Satellite were still enough to hear the leaves on the trees rustle in a strong breeze.

"Have you ever been to Cleveland?" Tom asked.

"Never been outside of the boroughs."

"A borough?" Tom's eyes were enlarged by curiosity.

"What's a borough? this Kid asks. A borough," Fox enunciated, "is like a warren for humans, only aboveground, and everyone does their business, whatever it is, out in the open, and they don't care who sees 'em. I don't know how they do it in Cleveland or Satellite, but here the rabbits run quick and loose, and they're much harder to catch. I'll bet the rabbits in your town don't hop so fast, eh?"

"Well, everything is a little slower back home."

Fox grinned. "That's what I figured. Well, pretty soon little rabbit, you'll be running too. It's a faster world up here."

Tom didn't want to say it, but he didn't like the reality of a faster pace yet. "I'll get used to it, I'm sure."

"Some do and some don't, Kid. This city is a grinder, but just keep up with it and you won't get chewed up."

Tom nodded, not knowing what to say. Fox reminded him more of a character in a book than a real person so far.

"Ah, you all look alike when you first come here. You're all a little peaked when you arrive to Lady Liberty's streets."

"How far do we have to drive?"

"Not far, but in this city, a few blocks can take an hour."

"Who are we watching tonight?"

"Lady V, the junkies call 'er. Dorothy Calhoun—that's her real name. The 'V' is for Valium, but she's been piping heroin into the neighborhoods lately. I've been trailing her for two years now. We don't want the Lady, though, we want her King—he's the big fish."

"So, you help the police a lot?"

"Try to. This city is burning like Charleston. Race riots. Gang wars. Serial killers. Police don't have time for hot and cold drug cases like this, so here I am."

"I didn't know it was so bad up here."

"Well, it is. You'll see."

Tom was a little afraid he would.

"So, how often do you watch Lady V?

"Less and less often. I don't have the time I used to."

Tom looked at Fox's face. Its features disappeared into a new darkness outside. The wagon crept through buildings and people that seemed to be made of the night itself instead of light and color and noise, which Tom thought the entire city produced around the clock.

The wagon stopped. Fox dimmed the lights.

"She lives here?"

"Up there."

'Up there' was a corner apartment on the eighth floor of a nondescript brownstone.

Lady V's apartment was partially lit, but it was a still light. Lady V had either gone out or gone to sleep.

"It's Saturday. She'll be making drops. Should be back by ten." Fox settled comfortably into his seat as if he were in his living room watching television.

Fox closed his eyes. "Let me know when she shows up."

Tom's nerves bounced.

"Are you sure...uh..."

"You'll be fine. Just wake me, Kid. I almost forgot." Fox reached into the backseat, which had disappeared in the darkness, and retrieved an old camera from a hidden, zippered compartment inside the seat. The camera's cloth strap looked nearly eaten all the way through with wear at the spot where it was intended to hang over a shoulder. "You ever used a camera?"

Tom nodded.

"Okay, so this'll be simple. Hold it like this, and just point and adjust the focus like this, and click this button to take the picture. But, only take a picture if you see something important."

Tom pulled the strap over his head. It seemed like too much responsibility too soon. But he knew he was a solo pilot when the snoring began.

For more than an hour, Tom watched the light in Lady V's apartment. Fox remained untouched in his netherworld of dreams. At 10:05, Lady V's light switched off.

Tom woke Fox.

"Huh? What?" With eyes open, but not fully awake, Fox snorted through his nose one last time.

"She went to bed, I think." Tom felt himself getting sleepy just thinking about it.

Fox yawned and rubbed his head. "Good job, Kid." Fox sat back up in his seat and fumbled for the key in the ignition.

"That's it?" Tom asked, his eyes enlarging with incredulity.

"That's it, Kid. You'll come back tomorrow night and sit in this wagon again. Your training is officially over."

"But, what happens if I see something?" Tom's voice sounded panicked.

"Then, you'll tail Lady V as best you can." Fox glanced at his protégé whose face had contorted.

"Look, I've done it for more than thirty years. I started when the Sicilians and Jews were still running the big syndicates. I've seen it all. I wasn't much older than you." Fox's bloodshot eyes latched onto Tom, as if they could somehow transfer all the wisdom and experience of three decades.

"But, what if..."

"Let the 'what if's' work themselves out on the job. It's the only way in this business."

Tom slumped down in his seat beneath the weight of so many questions he couldn't ask. He allowed himself to become lost in the dark streets leading away from Lady V's home which eventually merged again with the chaotic fusion of human and electro-mechanical energies, charging up the city through the night.

"Get some sleep. Tomorrow, we'll process you for a license, and you'll be official, Kid. Once you see that card, you'll feel better."

Tom's spirits lifted at the mention of a license.

Fox left Tom to the old brown couch in his office and slipped upstairs to his apartment. Tom closed his eyes, but he didn't fall asleep. The thought of how far he had traveled from home in just one day and night kept him awake.

Tom rubbed his thumb over the laminated surface of his new P.I. license. His soft face and eyes stared back at him from beneath the glossy plastic. He was too clean, he thought. He wished he at least had a voice like Fox's. Maybe he would start smoking.

After a quick dinner at Fox's preferred luncheonette in Hell's Kitchen, Fox gave Tom the keys to the wagon and a spare key to his office. "You need to make friends with this city. Best way to do that is learning its anatomy. I wrote down the directions to V's. I'll take the subway home."

Tom gulped. "Okay."

"You'll be fine, Kid. And I've got a good lead on a shipment of coke coming in for a guy I've been tracking. Here's a few dimes if you see anything. I don't answer, keep trying. Lady V has never been in earlier than ten on my watch. There's always a first time, of course."

Fox's last words felt like a premonition.

"Thanks for the dimes."

"You're welcome, Kid."

Tom watched Fox disappear into the landscape of the city.

He read the directions Fox had scrawled hastily on a grubby diner receipt.

It took more than two hours and four stops to ask for clarification of Fox's scrawl before Tom reached Lady V's building.

It was dark by then, at a little past eight. Tired, Tom closed his eyes for a moment. A moment of dreaming about the spring sunshine met through the stained glass windows of the library in Satellite stretched into an hour-and-a-half nap.

Even though the dream was pleasant, Tom woke up with sweat on his skin. He wiped his forehead with his sleeve. To his relief, the light was still on in Lady V's apartment. He checked his watch. It read 9:45. At 10:05, the lights were still on, but someone appeared in the window for an instant. It wasn't long enough for Tom to discern much except a medium-build, medium-height female, with a long, thick black ponytail gathered high on the woman's head. The light remained on this time. And, ten minutes later, Lady V slipped out of her apartment building and around the corner.

Tom's thoughts stumbled over one another. He couldn't focus. But, he managed to start the car and turn on the lights, creeping along the street like Fox did, hoping to see where Lady V went. By the time Tom reached the side street where Lady V had turned, it looked as if she had never been there. Tom drove down the street anyway, but his target had vanished, and he had even forgotten to pull out the camera. He had failed his first test as an investigator.

Tom slowly made his way back to Fox's apartment. He was afraid to face his new boss, but instead of confronting the older man, Tom found a policeman banging on Fox's office door.

"Uh, are you looking for Mr. Manus?"

The officer, who stood well over six feet tall and in athletic shape, swung around. A dark brown, handlebar mustache aged him beyond his otherwise youthful presentation.

"Who are you?" the officer asked, moving closer to Tom.

"I'm Fox's—Mr. Manus'—new assistant. Tom Reiger."

Tom extended his hand, but the officer was in no mood as he maintained arms folded across his broad chest.

"I'm Officer Connelly. Maybe you can help me."

"Sure." Tom nodded.

"You're not from around here are you?"

Tom shook his head.

"Where's your boss?"

Tom reflexively answered, considering it was a police officer questioning him.

"He said he was following up on a lead."

As soon as Tom said it, he regretted it. Fox said he worked with the police, but maybe not this one.

"A lead? The only lead your boss is following up on comes inside a bottle. That old man filling your head with bullshit is just a fucking drunk. You should go back where you came from. There's nothing for you with that old man. He was supposed to meet me tonight in Queens. That's the lead right there. I was supposed to make detective. Fuck that Fox."

The officer punched Fox's office door enough to leave a dent. It startled Tom. He wasn't used to such a physical reaction.

"You tell your boss he won't work any more cases with the Twenty-Fourth no more. You hear that Manus?" The officer threw his voice angrily at an anonymous place in the air of the hallway.

Tom could only nod. The whole night had been a disaster. *Was it true? Was Fox a broken-down alcoholic?* Tom was tired and wanted to sleep. Fox had turned off the lights. Tom wanted to fling himself onto the musty, leather couch and close his eyes, escaping into warm, sunny memories of home. But, before he could reach the couch, he stumbled over something in the middle of the floor. It was large and unevenly shaped, and it moaned. It was Fox.

"Ooohhh, whydya do that, huh?" Fox gave off a thick alcoholic stench. The smell sent Tom reeling backward.

"Where's your light switch?"

Thankfully, the only clutter Fox accumulated was in the form of glass bottles, which were all neatly stashed in a rubbish bin. A good five minutes passed before the torch lamps sputtered fully awake.

Fox's face was a mash of emotions. His mouth spread across the face with an unnatural giddiness. It had the superficial effect of something inhuman, and yet it transmitted unwelcome intimacy and vulnerability that Tom was unprepared for from his new boss.

"You missed it. You missed a meetup with an officer— the one who just gave your door a shiner." Tom's voice sounded almost stern. "I lost Lady V tonight. I had her but I lost her down some street."

Fox's expression emptied of all emotion save regret. His eyes filled and snot bubbled at his nostrils. He covered his face protectively with his arms.

Tom felt sorry for Fox. Tom had come all this way for nothing. Fox shook with quiet anguish until he became still, other than air blowing his nostrils wide with snoring. Tom covered him with a blanket and managed to shove a pillow under his head.

There was nothing for Tom to do but get some sleep. In the morning, he would return to Satellite. There would only be the tale of a sad, old man, and maybe he would keep that to himself. Tom threw himself on the couch and shut his eyes against the strange night.

◆ ◆ ◆

Tom woke to something spectral hovering over him in the bleak light of dusk. It was Fox. Tom jumped. Fox's eyes were serious, but dry and calm. Tom decided not to disclose what the cop had told him.

"You must still have a pocketful of dimes, eh?" Fox pulled back a ratty muslin curtain hanging across one window in the room and stared outside, but Tom sensed he wasn't looking for anything.

"Uh, yeah. I never called." Tom ran a hand through his bed-mussed hair. "I lost Lady V. I saw her leaving and tried to follow her, but... Tom trailed off, hoping to arrive more quickly at the inevitable reprimand. Fox continued staring out the window.

"Kid, you're a shiny new penny. I don't expect you to plug right in and light up. You'll keep on this case."

Tom's eyes protested. "Look, I'm not cut out for this. After last night, I realized I should be back in Satellite, and..."

Fox didn't let Tom finish.

"You just need some time on the streets. Don't let me down, okay?" His eyes emphasized his last several words. Tom felt drawn in again. This broken-down man was still fighting for something.

"Okay." Tom nodded.

"No Lady V tonight. There's a guy in SOHO selling art, but it ain't just art. He's delivering coke, heroin, angel dust, fairy dust—or whatever else his customers ask for—in the backs of these paintings. We need his supplier or suppliers. Anyway, let's go get some salt and grease. I've got a headache that calls for eggs and ham steak."

Tom, by now practiced in shedding the hundred questions that arose each time Fox opened his mouth, dutifully followed the older man out the door. After a greasy plate of overly salted food in a diner a few blocks from Fox's building, Fox took Tom up in the Statue of Liberty.

"That's where my grandparents came through in the last century." Fox pointed out Ellis Island. "You know that rundown church next door to me? They used to take me there when I was just a kid."

The gruffness in Fox's voice mellowed as he spoke of his distant past. "That's why I live and work where I do. I don't go to Mass no more, but it's nice to know God is next door, and maybe, just maybe he still watches over me."

"Why did you become a P.I.?" Tom asked.

It was obvious by the quizzical look on Fox's face that no one, including himself, had ever asked why.

"Malachi O'Shay." Fox nodded. His face flushed with enlightenment, his eyes brightening with excitement Tom had not seen before. "He was a cousin of a cousin of a cousin—just like I'm your friend of a friend of a friend. Anyway, he was a beat cop who turned P.I. just before the big boom dropped on all the heads on Wall Street. Uncly Mally—that's what I called him—was good friends with my pop. He would tell me all these stories about Luciano, Masseria, Genovese—all these wise guys. He helped the cops with these guys, but he didn't have to hassle with so many rules. For him, this city was the Wild West. Now, there's too many damn rules." Fox shrugged. "Well, anyway, he was the one who helped me get set up. God rest him." Fox turned his glance from the harbor to Tom. "What about you?"

"Me?" Tom thought for a moment. "I guess I wanted to live what I read. I got tired of reading about other people living life."

"See these?" Fox lifted up his rumpled navy blue suit jacket to reveal a series of scars on his stomach and chest. "That's living life. I'm not trying to scare ya, Kid, but maybe I am, just a little."

Tom swallowed, meditating on Fox's scars. He would probably never know these flesh stories.

The afternoon faded. Fox and Tom ate an early dinner of tuna salad sandwiches at another diner counter and returned to Fox's building. Fox again handed Tom the keys, and all Tom could think of was the old man passed out on the floor.

"Here's the directions to SOHO. You've got those dimes and my number—oh, and the camera."

Tom nodded. "Yep. I'll call if I see anything. Promise."

Tom made his way to an area dead to its previous existence as a booming nexus of textile production, searching for the gallery that sold more than art. The gallery turned out to be inside an old warehouse. It appeared to be so exclusive there was no name on the outside, only a street number stenciled in white against the blue building above the door, which was painted a lusty red.

Tom parked across the street from the gallery and waited. It was getting dark. He had become a creature that waited for the moon, not for the sun. Sunlight was a prelude to the new driving forces in his life.

The red door opened and a man appeared with wild black hair that reminded Tom of cattails blowing in the wind near the edge of a pond; wispy at the tips, but thickening down toward the roots. Lanky, thin, and gaunt in the face, the man looked older than his youthful abundance of hair suggested. He wore an expensive looking white suit and circular spectacles. Tom snapped several pictures.

The man's eyes were cast down the block and lit up behind their glasses when a woman, as sleek and striking in her proportions as any glory of modern architecture, clicked out her emphatic, red-heeled stride toward the gallery owner. Tom found the owner's name beneath Fox's directions: RENSON STIGLER.

For nearly three hours, a continuous supply of patrons entered through the red door. Each left with something to alter and expand their minds, Tom thought. The camera flashed several more times before Renson locked the red door and walked away from the gallery. Tom turned the ignition and followed Stigler, who had slipped down an alley on the right a few blocks away. Stigler escaped into a door in the alley that appeared to lead into an abandoned building. Tom saw no signage, or anything else, to acknowledge the dirty, gray structure was anything but forgotten.

He found a payphone half a block away. He dialed Fox's number, letting the phone ring at least ten times. He wondered whether his boss was already passed out on the floor. Tom recycled the same dime two more times before giving up.

He returned to the wagon, and retrieved a small notepad from his back jeans pocket. In high school, he had used the pad to scribble quotes for newspaper stories for the school paper. Maybe his well-honed note taking and observational skills would at last be used for something more substantial than covering the construction of a new school gymnasium.

His hands shaking, Tom locked the wagon and began walking toward the door in the alley. He had no way of knowing how far inside Renson had gone—or who he intended to meet—if he was meeting anyone at all. There were windows in the building, but they had been covered in black plastic.

Tom walked all the way around the building and noticed three entrances—all locked. He saw a fire escape. The building wasn't that high, so he pulled down the fire escape ladder and started to climb. He was young, limber, and not too far removed from summer afternoons in Satellite, scaling tall, venerable Maples with his best friend, Joe Legrange. Tom reached the roof, and a nearly full moon offered enough light for him to find the door. Tom pulled on it as he had the other three, but this one opened.

He found no light to guide him down the stairwell. As he descended into complete darkness, his own imagination burdened his mission, taunting him with nothing more than dark air.

At last, he found the landing which led immediately to another door. To Tom's surprise, it also opened. A paler shade of darkness greeted him through this door as the windows on the highest floor—a large open space of glass and concrete—were not covered by plastic. Tom noticed only one other door, and again, it opened into a stubborn blackness. Tom persisted and made it to the lowest level.

An adrenalized sweat covered him by the time he reached the bottom. Beyond a single revolution of the doorknob were muffled voices and a light softly bleaching a wide darkness.

Tom crept toward the light emitted from a narrow window over an office door at the other end of the oceanic darkness. He felt for the camera around his neck, reassuring himself of its presence, as he waded through the thinning darkness. He found the face of the office door, flattening his body against it. The voices were loud and the door was thin. Tom heard a feminine tone first.

"I can't believe I stayed in nursing for so long. Nurses aren't respected. I get more respect from my junkies—now they're fucking loyal."

Lady V. Tom shivered. *So, Stigler and Lady V used the same supplier.*

One of the men began talking. The voice was male, but softly coaxing the way it lingered on certain words.

"Dottie, you should get down to see my operation. I still say we would be *gaaangbusters* together, but you *sooo* love tending to your little unkempt urchins."

"They're my children—the only ones I'll ever have—and could ever stand. Renny can't stand the poor unwashed masses, can you dear?"

A second man spoke with a nuanced, Mexican accent. His tone sounded cold and detached from the friendly rhythm of conversation shared between Lady V and Renson Stigler.

"We need to leave soon if we are to meet Manuel before he leaves for Chile. He will have something very special for both of you to take back to your clients. The stuff they are growing now in Mexico is more pure than anything you've seen up here yet."

"Our ship has come in at last, Dottie Girl," the flamboyant voice bounced.

"Don't you fuckin' know it, Ren." Lady V giggled. Her tone was too rough for such a girlish response.

Tom skittered like an insect to the side of the office, which was a free-standing box, waiting for the trio to exit. As soon as he heard the door to the outside slam, he bolted toward the door.

Lady V, Stigler and their supplier slipped into a black Chrysler Imperial. Tom clicked the camera several times before jumping in Fox's wagon. He caught up with the supplier's car, remaining at an innocent distance.

Tom realized the city was long gone a couple of hours later when he was still driving. By the time the Imperial pulled over at a gas station in Pennsylvania, Tom convinced himself he was already too invested to turn back.

He followed the sleek black car back onto the road and settled into the cross-country driver's trance. He only stopped when the Chrysler stopped. This included a stay at two seedy motels along the way in Indiana and Oklahoma, where he attempted to contact Fox on a parking lot pay phone several times to no avail. He called his parents, too, but they were out each time, most likely having cocktails with the Millers next door or at the movies.

Tom barely slept. For three nights he followed the Imperial from New York City to the Mexico border, for fear his targets would wake earlier than him and he would lose them. So, he stayed up writing down everything he had seen in detail on his notepad.

By the time border agents were displayed in glass and metal boxes, Tom was too tired to protest, and anyway he had come too far to show Fox empty hands. It was a huge risk leaving the country, and his nerves told him so from head to toe, but he focused on the possible reward of the arrest of Lady V and her cohorts. Tom would call his boss as soon as he was in Mexico.

Tom passed over the border with ease. He felt a little concerned about the return trip, but he would worry about that when the time came.

Tom first viewed Juarez at sunset. The city sprawled all the way into the cold grey of the mountains, warmed by the sky's oranges, reds and purples. Tom locked his car doors as Juarez came fully alive at its core with swarms of motorcycles darting like fireflies around Tom's car, and a constant commotion of voices, bodies and vehicles exploding all around him with a greater intensity even than New York City. Here and there streetlights spotlighted less-than-savory scenarios such as women selling their flesh as if by the pound and children with tired eyes soliciting passing adults with a constant rant in a language he wish he understood for 'God knows what,' Tom thought. Tom continued to follow Lady V and Stigler through the city, more concerned now with maintaining a tight gap than arousing suspicion.

The supplier's car passed through the dense core of Juarez like a large kidney stone through the body, but finally entered an area with less traffic. The air thinned out of voices and motorcycle growls, and the space between buildings grew as more wealth painted a cleaner, newer gloss over homes and businesses. When Tom noticed the Imperial turning down a long road off the main highway, he switched off his lights before following.

At the end of the gravel road, which turned out to be about half-mile long, stood a large house. Tom could see the lights on in every room. The supplier parked in a semi-circle drive. Tom watched all three passengers walk to the front door. A large, dark man silhouetted in bright light greeted his guests.

Tom waited for the door to close and continued slowly up the long road, his heart trying to escape the moment by pounding out an exit from inside his chest. He turned off the ignition, got out, and began walking.

The air felt warm and humid, but not intolerable. A dog howled in the distance. Other sounds of the city were lost to the wide-open night, blank other than winking starlight.

Tom peered through the first window he came to, but there was nothing to see other than gaudy yellow, orange and pink walls, floor and furniture hues clawing at his eyes.

The next window caused Tom to duck. A gathering had formed in tackily executed, though plush, surroundings. Lady V wore a tight, red pantsuit with a sheen rivaled only by that of her long, black hair pulled into a high ponytail. Her skin was alabaster, and her eyes the lightest blue Tom had ever seen. She had a fine bone structure. Tom was surprised to see such aesthetic elegance in the face of a woman who sold pills and heroin to junkies. Renson sat next to Lady V on a vanilla-colored loveseat, legs crossed, delicately clasping a green-colored cocktail that more closely resembled a fairytale potion.

The expiring supplier, who looked average in every way, sat in a chair on one side of Renson and Lady V. With mostly Indian features, there was nothing remarkable in the Mexican's face other than the deadness of his brown-black eyes. They evoked nothing human. He smoked a cigar and waited to pass his symbolic torch to the man sitting across from him in a chair with an ornate wooden back as high as or higher than most monarchic thrones.

Even sitting, Manuel was an imposing man. Unlike the old dealer, Manuel's face conjured up images of refined Spanish conquistadores. His skin was lighter than the other supplier. He wore his black hair pulled back into a low braid at his neck, and a long purple tunic shirt hung over black dress pants. His light brown eyes registered more activity than the other supplier. Callous amusement filled them.

Tom pulled up his camera and focused the lens on the scene before him. After snapping several shots, he returned to the wagon. He could not believe his ease in collecting evidence. It was somewhat unsettling.

He found his way back to the heart of Juarez. He noticed a payphone alongside the road but wasn't sure it would work or take American currency. Luckily, it did. From what he had seen of Juarez, he didn't want to linger a second longer than it took to update Fox. Tom almost wished the booth were cloaked in darkness instead of illuminated by a street lamp that in Tom's mind only alerted the locals to his foreign presence, which may or may not be welcome.

On the fifth ring, Fox picked up.

"Mexico?"

Even over the phone Tom could smell the whiskey. After the word 'Mexico', most of what came out of Fox was incoherent. The older man sounded upset with Tom, but the particulars weren't clear. Tom let Fox rant.

Tom said goodbye and hung up the phone, as pesos cascaded into a metal slot. He had never seen a Mexican coin. They were bronze with Spanish words and mysterious and ancient-looking symbols. He rubbed his finger over the raised ridges of these symbols. In his momentary distraction, a grizzled, old Mexican man with long, matted gray and black hair approached Tom. His skin was dark and weathered and he wore a strap around his own neck, but it was connected to a shallow wooden box that held more than ten clear glass bottles of varying sizes. They all appeared to contain the same dark, amber liquid.

"Tequila?"

Tom should have guessed tequila before the man spoke. He had never seen it, but he had heard it described years before by a childhood friend who had visited Mexico with his family. The friend had sent him a postcard with a mule sitting next to a stereotypical Mexican in a big yellow sombrero at a tequila bar, and the mule was drinking too. Tom started to talk himself out of a taste of the liquor. After all, he was in another country and he needed to stay alert to his surroundings. On the other hand, he couldn't leave Mexico without at least trying its infamous liquor.

"How much?" Tom held up one finger.

The old man pointed at the change in Tom's hand and took a few coins, presenting Tom with the largest bottle in his box.

"*Bebe!*" The old man shouted at Tom, simulating a generous swig, tilting his own wrinkled head back.

Tom smiled. He nodded and toasted himself and his strange cross-country adventure before swallowing his first taste. The tequila aroused euphoric warmth throughout his body, so he took another long drink, hoping to increase the sensation. He nearly stumbled off his feet, and he would have, had it not been for the old vendor who bade him sit down on the crudely poured sidewalk. He smiled at the old man and drank until the colors and objects and people around him shifted like a kaleidoscope.

His thoughts bobbed loosely, breaking apart against one another in his brain. Images of his parents and his old neighborhood in Satellite and the library fused and unfused. He closed his eyes. When he opened them, there was a blank space where Fox's wagon had been. Tom's eyes widened. *The keys were still in his pocket, but where was the car?*

"The wagon. Dammit!" Tom put his hands on his head, his eyes wild with panic. He wanted to cry and scream at the same time. He stared at the tequila. It had betrayed him, yet, it seemed like his only friend. His mind and body were moving through quicksand.

He filled his body with more of the liquid heat. He drank until he was the center of a carousel around which the world was heavily and slowly spinning. At some point, he levitated. Or perhaps mysterious hands carried him. Then he vaguely perceived riding in a car up a steep incline to a very dark, cool place. There, at last, he lay his head against something hard that smelled like rain and iron.

He passed into a netherworld of slumber. In Tom's dream, Fox was trying to find him, as were his parents. Even Tom's old friend, Joe Granger, was calling for him like he used to when he wanted Tom to come out and play in his tree house or go fishing on a Saturday morning. They all wandered together through an open clearing, surrounded by trees. Tom called back to each of them, but they couldn't hear him. Then, the old man who had sold him tequila found him again and tried to sell him more tequila, but when Tom went to pay the man, the tequila had disappeared, along with the wooden box around the man's neck, and the old man was running into a dark woods saying the tequila could only be sold at night and daybreak was coming fast. The old man called to Tom to follow him into the wood, or else he would die. Tom didn't want to die, but he couldn't move. He tried to follow the old man, but the wood seemed to get farther and farther away. He yelled after the old man to wait for him, but he was long gone. A blinding, white light burned through the wood and Tom thrashed and struggled to move.

He woke to his heart beating furiously. His body ached. He tried to move, but his neck and back failed to cooperate. Though painful, Tom was finally able to lift his upper body so he could sit up. His head ached and he was dizzy. He recalled the tequila and the car ride. The light that had pierced his subconscious streamed in from outside the cave where he had passed out.

Someone had dumped him like refuse. He remembered the car rising to a higher altitude. Tom stood up, and though his legs were alternatingly stiff and wobbly, he made his way to the cave opening. The dream he had just had was more believable than the view of an endless expanse of canyons repeating itself infinitely to an unreachable horizon. *Someone had left him here, but why?* His wallet was gone, as were the car keys. He started to shake as if he were cold, but the air was still hot. He forced his thoughts away from panic and his body eventually followed, his shaking calming down. A petty thief wouldn't have gone to the trouble of bringing him all the way out to a remote canyon cave.

Tom thought of how simple it had been to follow the supplier's car all the way to Mexico, and then to Manuel's home. Fox had followed Lady V for years and hadn't come up with any remotely promising leads in all that time. Tom had been able to tail her almost as soon as arriving in New York City from Small Townville, USA. after observing her for a couple of nights. *Had it all been a set up?* The thought antagonized him, but the question, it seemed, would have to wait for the answer before it could be asked.

Tom surveyed the landscape—grateful he was young and in good physical shape.

He stretched first as if preparing for a run as he had back home at least three times a week during track practice. He didn't know in which direction to start moving, but he did know he had to move or he would die in this wilderness. He started climbing over the unforgiving terrain.

His pace was slow and awkward, especially without the incentive of a firm direction to motivate the body through the mind. If there was a road or a path, Tom figured he was moving away from it. He hadn't seen anything resembling either after several hours.

He stopped to rest in another cave. He hadn't moved much at all. His hands were scraped from grabbing at rough brush to pull himself along, and he started to feel weak from dehydration. All the tequila he had drunk didn't help. He needed to continue on.

He got no further than the mouth of cave when something small and fast exploded against the entrance. Tom jumped back into the cave. *Someone was hunting him.*

Tom lay in mental and physical paralysis, denying his situation, but there was no denying the hot lead that sizzled in his gut. Warm blood seeped from his side through his shirt. He was surprised it felt no different than warm water against his hand. At one point, he fell asleep and dreamt of being back at the library in Satellite, but the librarian wouldn't let him have his old job back. She said there were no guns allowed in the library, and Tom felt a pistol belted at his side. He tried to climb onto the library roof. He remembered a way to get in, as he'd snuck in one time through the roof door when he had forgotten his key. But, in his dream, the roof was made entirely of clear glass. As he tried to move across it, the glass began cracking like a pond of ice. It gave way beneath him and he fell through.

Just before Tom hit the ground amidst all the glass, he woke up to his own body gasping for life, as if he had hit the broken, glassy roof of the library after all. He looked up and saw the old man who sold him the tequila. The old man mixed Spanish with English as he spoke.

"You should have stayed in that first cave. *Tu eres muy joven.* You're only a boy, and I'm trained to take a life, no matter if it's *viejo o joven.* You should have never come down here, little *gringo.*"

An old man with a brown face, white hair, and wide Indian features stood over him, going in and out of focus. His arms hung casually, almost limply at his side, despite the pistol that faintly smoked in his right hand.

Even the English words the old man spoke were muddled in Tom's dying mind. The oxygen leaked rapidly from his thoughts. They deflated. He couldn't get enough air. His last thoughts were of his parents and Fox. He had let Fox down. He should never have left Satellite.

The old Mexican gently closed Tom's eyes and covered the body with an old wool blanket. The old man would have to come back with younger men to move the body. He shook his head as he walked back toward the cave entrance. Maybe he wouldn't let anyone else touch the body. It wouldn't be right. He had killed the boy. He was a beat-up, old *sicario*, but he would move the body and bury the young man as he had always handled his bodies himself.

◆ ◆ ◆

Two months later, Fox looked around his apartment one last time, making sure he didn't leave anything. He remembered the box of files in his office downstairs. He found the box and couldn't help but open it. After all, it had been the last case he had worked just before his official retirement.

Typed in all capital letters on the front label, was THE REIGER FILE. Fox opened the cardboard box of files and out spilled the photos Tom had taken of Lady V, Renson Stigler, Manuel Santiago and Ramirez, the former supplier.

Tom's body had been found buried in the Chihuahuan Desert after Santiago gave up his hit man during an interrogation conducted by Juarez police. Fox's eyes glistened as he read Tom's name on his former trainee's P.I. license.

Fox saw the *New York Times'* photo of Tom's parents receiving a medal on Tom's behalf from the FBI and New York Police Department for his photographic evidence and notes that lead to the convictions of Lady V, Stigler, Santiago and Ramirez. Underneath the photo was a newspaper article about

Officer Bobby Connelly's arrest for taking bribes from Lady V. Fox also noted a picture depicting the arrest of Stigler for acting as an accomplice in Tom's disappearance.

Fox smiled, but his eyes filled with tears when he saw the old camera and Tom's notebook, found by petty thieves who had stripped the car and discovered both in the hidden compartment of his station wagon abandoned outside of Juarez by one of Santiago's handlers. Fox had been smart to label the camera with his name and phone number. The pawnbroker who purchased the camera from the thieves had been generously rewarded for turning the camera over to Fox. Lucky for Fox, the car thieves had not thought to look for the critical film inside, and even luckier, the pawnbroker decided to circumvent the normal channels of justice since the broker knew the Juarez police would not have offered him any reward for what was most certainly a gringo's stolen camera. No one he knew was named 'Fox' or had a New York City area code. The broker gambled on a long-distance call to Fox.

The only photo absent was one of Tom. Those bastards in their Chrysler had dragged the poor Kid all the way across the country for slaughter. Connelly had tailed Tom even as he tailed Lady V. Fox shook his head. Tom's Achilles' heel had been his youthful passion for his work—a passion long expired inside Fox.

He closed the file, and then closed his office door for good.

A NIGHT WITH KALI

Rita Banerjee

TAMAL-DA KNEW all the back roads of Kolkata. He never made mistakes. He arrived at appointments early, even during storms and through the monsoon season.

He was a taxi driver, and he shuttled me from Salt Lake to College Street via Dakshinapan on a particularly rainy day in mid-July. The Kolkata sky, usually dimly lit in dry weather with layers of dust, smoke, and exhaust blurring out the mid-day sun, had turned a quiet and ominous shade. Coupled with the pollution and the water-stained facades of buildings, the sky looked like an amorphous slump of gray with a few ambiguous white clouds trailing shadows in their wake.

Despite the weather Tamal-da sounded optimistic.

"Don't worry, didi," he said, smiling into the mirror, his moon face framed by thick glasses. "We'll make it in time." We were rushing to College Street to pick up the latest collection of poetry by a former Marxist poet. I had just finished interviewing him in his stylish flat in Salt Lake with Tamal-da serving as my makeshift cameraman. He worked well under pressure. He moonlighted as my right-hand man when I needed him. And thankfully, he had not questioned my sanity today when I had requested to go searching for an obscure book of poetry in the middle of a heavy rainstorm in the middle of a month-long monsoon in Kolkata.

The sky hissed and snapped above us. The rain plunked down on our taxicab as if the roof was meant to be a snare-drum. The water created an endless, but unhurried, drumbeat.

To cross town from Salt Lake to reach College Street, Tamal-da had taken a few of the major overpasses at first. But the overpasses were unusually busy, congested with cars and people who wanted to get home. So near the shopping district of Dakshinapan, Tamal-da had decided to get off the main ramp and take a few by-ways to reach the bookstore faster.

Heading out of the bumper-to-bumper traffic, we did well at first. The Kolkata roads and alleyways, which were normally full of motorbikes, tourists, sometimes goats or cattle, and much of the time full of smoky lorries and speeding busses, looked desolate and almost abandoned. A few people walked through streams of dirty water, some using books and shawls as makeshift umbrellas. Others stood elevated on the concrete steps of old buildings trying to beckon the few rickshaw-wallahs who dared to brave the rain. Some of the rickshaw-wallahs hesitated, unsure if crossing the knee-deep currents would be worth the fare of an extra customer or two.

For the most part, the roadside fruit and vegetable stands and chai stalls had shut down as had the newspaper. It looked like most of the remaining people on the streets were either trying to rush home or trying to rush to cover.

We didn't meet any thrill-seekers until a few streets down.

"Hey," Tamal-da interrupted my train of thought, "I think I know a quick way to College Street from here."

"Okay, let's go," I said. It felt like an underwater adventure to navigate the streets this way on a mid-summer's day.

Everything started off fine as we followed the small roads running parallel to the overpass. But then Tamal-da began to wind his taxi through the narrow gullies between apartment buildings and behind storefronts.

The houses in these neighborhoods were shuttered. On the second and third floor balconies of many of the buildings, thin strands of rope jerked violently in the wind. The clotheslines would normally be full of the day's laundry, but they were left limp and forgotten during the monsoon.

The rain fell so heavily it was difficult to distinguish clear shapes through the taxi windows, which had become opaque, moving rivers.

"Hey, look," I pointed as Tamal-da tried to steer through a particularly treacherous road. "Are those boys actually playing in the water?"

Many meters in front of us, a group of young teenage boys were causing a ruckus on the street. One of the boys, surely the ringleader, had dared to traverse the flooded street on a rickety old bicycle. His friend had jumped on the seat behind him hoping, perhaps, to catch a fun-free ride. But as the boys moved forward in the water-clogged streets, the water level began to increase.

Now not only had the water risen to the top of the wheels of the bike, but the front wheel had gotten stuck in some kind of mud or sharp object on the street.

While the ringleader of the group was amused and laughing off his predicament, his companion looked deathly afraid of the rising water. He had almost climbed up onto the wire rack attached to the back of the bicycle seat, and he looked like he would swan-dive into the river below if he wasn't so afraid of the murky water.

A stone throw away stood a third, younger boy watching the progress of his friends. He laughed uncontrollably at the absurdity of the situation and appeared to offer no help.

Watching the boys through the rain-stained window, I smiled slightly, amused at their comedy of errors. I didn't even notice Tamal-da's car heading in their direction, crossing parallel to their bike, until it was too late.

"I can make it over," Tamal-da muttered under his breath.

He jerked the car forward on the waterlogged streets. The water slid over the tops of our tires and over the front bumper. The engine, cranked up to the max, whinnied in complaint. Our Ambassador, the old beast, was trying to push through the flooded alley, to no avail.

The wheels of the car were first rolling in knee-deep water, lurching in jerky spurts across the road. In the distance, a small corner street was visible as the old cab hurtled towards it. But even its thick tires were no match for the rising, rapid yellow-brown currents running through the streets. Soon a small sliver of beige water marked a streak across the black leather floor of the Ambassador. Following it, a choppy wave of muddied water snuck in through the cracks at the bottom of the door.

"Tamal-da," I shrieked, lifting my feet up and crossing them in the backseat. I placed the few bags of books we had procured up on the seat next to me, hoping the water would not rise up and devour us.

"Don't worr—." Whatever Tamal-da was going to say in reassurance died on his lips as the engine sputtered and groaned. The cab, fighting a losing battle, swayed one last time and then shuttered to an undignified halt.

Stuck in the middle of the gully with the engine dead, the brown water trickled into the cab and rose at a steady pace until it made a firm splash just underneath the backseat.

"Do something!" I yelled, raising myself to sit on the headboard and moving everything up to the back windowsill.

"Don't—"

"Forget don't worry!" I said with rising anxiety. "We're going to drown! We're going to drown if we stay like this!"

"But, didi," Tamal-da said, sitting Buddha-like with his legs folded on the front seat, "the water has stopped coming in. And look," he pointed, "help is on the way."

Peeking out from my crouched position, I noticed the three hooligans from the street coming towards us.

"Oh, great," I muttered.

The boys half-paddled, half-bounced through the street to reach us. It seemed like the middle boy who had been so afraid of falling into the water from his bicycle seat was swimming through the gully like a baby seal. So much for theatrics.

When they reached us, grinning, Tamal-da rolled down the window.

"Do you think you can push our car backwards a little?" he asked. "Backwards onto that rocky area over there." Tamal-da pointed to a relatively dry, unflooded spot to our left.

"Of course," said the ringleader. "Just stay there. Let us try to do it."

And with a bit of machismo and a whole lot of determination, the boys placed their hands on front of the car.

"Okay," the ringleader shouted, "push when I say go. Ready? One, two, three, go!"

Bam!

Three pair of strong teenage hands shoved, and in no time our taxi was gliding backwards through the water like a captain-less schooner until it careened majestically onto the pile of bricks sticking out from the sidewalk to our left.

"Great," I grumbled as the cab formed a thirty-degree angle with its back-end up like a beached whale.

"At least the water can run out this way," Tamal-da said with a smile.

"Does the engine work?"

"No," he shook his head as he repeatedly tried to turn the engine with the key. "I'll ask the boys for help."

"Wait," I was about to say, but Tamal-da had already jumped out of his seat and stood outside in the now ankle-deep water, talking to the boys. They listened and nodded their heads gleefully and then after a few moments, went splashing into the water heading back in the direction of the last major intersection we had passed.

"Will they be back?" I asked, poking my head out of the rear window as I tried to balance myself on the angled seat.

"I think so," Tamal-da said, hands in his pockets.

"How can you be so sure?"

"Well," he said, pausing, "I promised to give them five hundred rupees if they came back with another taxi and got help."

"What! Do you think that'll actually work?"

"It should. It's a lot of money and they look like they could use it. But," he turned to me, "if you think they're unreliable, I could go get help myself."

"No way!" I said, "and leave me here? Just get back in so we can close the windows while we wait."

"Okay," he said.

Time passed slowly as we stared out at the intersection waiting for a sign of life or for the boys to come back. The sky echoed like a gong above us, and the rain picked up again, distorting the view from the window. I tried to distract myself from the growing chill in the cab by just talking.

"So Tamal-da," I asked, my breath materializing in the air, "where do you live?"

"In a small village outside of Kolkata."

"Does it take long to get there?"

"About two hours when the traffic is good."

"Why do you live so far away from the city?" I asked.

"Because I like rivers, and my house is near a river."

"Have you lived there all your life?"

"No, I moved there a few years ago."

"Oh," I paused. "Well, do you have anything interesting to say about the place where you live?" I asked, exhaling loudly and rubbing my arms to keep warm.

"Well," Tamal-da resumed his Buddha pose, "did I ever tell you the house I live in is haunted?"

"It is?" I asked, genuinely surprised.

"It depends on who you ask," he said. "But I can tell you the story if you like."

"Yes, please," I leaned forward to listen better.

"Hmm," he pondered, "where should I begin?"

◆ ◆ ◆

When I first moved to Kolkata, I was a teenager, a few months shy of fifteen. I didn't have a lot of relatives who lived in Kolkata, but I did have a few friends who had left our village near Krishnapur to find work in the city. It was through them that I got into the taxi business and was able to one day lease my own car. It took me a couple of years, but by the time I was in my early twenties, I was able to afford the rent for a small place of my own.

After searching for a few months, I finally found a place that felt like home to me. On the outskirts of Kolkata, I came across a small village-like community. There weren't many homes for rent there, but somehow I managed to convince the local foreman to show me an empty hut near the village river.

The hut had a thatched roof with a large interior room and small nooks for the bed and kitchen. It was the perfect size for me. The previous tenants had left behind an empty rattan cot standing upright on one of the interior walls and some steel plates and pots in the kitchen. The floors, too, had been left sparkling. They had been wiped completely clean like the walls. Though not much light came into the hut from the two main windows since the shutters had been kept tightly closed after the last tenants moved out, not much of the dust or dirt from the road had come in either. Sure there were a few cobwebs in the corners, and mosquitoes here and there, but small insects, like small pains, were to be expected.

As soon as I saw the beautiful river running behind the house from the tiny kitchen window, I knew I had to have the place. The river reminded me of home and the family I had left behind.

When I told the foreman this, he nodded but seemed hesitant to rent out the place to me. He suggested I might find a better, larger place if I waited just a bit longer.

But the hut was the perfect size for me, and it was in a secluded location clustered by large palm trees and bordered by the river. My only neighbor was a miller next door who processed rice and grain on the small stretch of land between our houses.

So I argued with the foreman, trying to convince him I would be an ideal tenant for such an ideal place. He still hesitated. He probably did not trust me since I was an outsider. I did not belong to the community, and he must have thought that because I was flashing around my money, I expected I could just live there.

After much debate and finagling over the price of the small cottage, we finally agreed on a monthly sum. The next day, I packed whatever utensils, small books, and clothes I owned and drove over my things from my friend's place in Kolkata to my newfound country home.

The village and the river proved to be a wonderful place to return to after work. None of my neighbors or townsfolk disturbed me. In fact, as the months wore on, I realized that no one in the small community would bother to talk to me at all. Even my neighbor, the miller, would regard me with disdain whenever I passed him on the street. His wife would scamper away if I ever met her during my walk to the village pump, and his children would cross themselves, mutter a prayer, or if really frightened, throw sticks at me before running away.

At first, I felt confused and then later, deeply hurt by this behavior. Did the villagers hate me so much because I was still seen by them as an outsider and as an unwanted interlocutor?

Disheartened, I would spend my very early mornings and late evenings at home and keep to myself when I was in the village.

One morning when I was getting ready for work and changing a tire on my cab, an unfamiliar middle-aged man walked up to me on the road at dawn.

He was looking for the miller. He said he was a local merchant. And hoping to do business with the miller, he had stopped by en route to the town next over.

Seeing me replace the tires on my cab, he asked me if I was a relative of the miller's—a nephew, perhaps?

"No," I answered. "I'm not related to the miller."

"But you live with him?" the merchant asked, rubbing his wool vest absently. "You are a friend? A guest in their house?"

"What? No." I laughed, picking up my wrench and wiping my forehead with a greasy cloth. "I live over there," I said, pointing to the cottage behind me.

The man's eyes widened, he sputtered, and then he stopped for a moment, smiling once again.

"Oh, you mean, you live on the other side of the village on the bank across the river," he nodded sympathetically.

"No, no," I said, slightly annoyed at his jumps in logic. "I live there, over there." I pointed to the large thatched hut behind us and turned back just in time to see the man's reaction.

"Oh, Ma Durga," he whispered, his eyes unusually wide all of a sudden.

"What?" I asked, startled by his strange behavior. I was going to ask him what was wrong when he began to back away from me.

"It..." he stuttered. "It was nice to meet you." He started to retreat backwards. "Take care. I must be on my way."

But before the man could flee, I ran up to him and caught him by the sleeves of his white pajama top.

"Wait," I said, forcing him to be still, "tell me what's wrong."

"Listen, bhai, I—"

"No," I nodded my head slowly, "tell me what's wrong with my house, and why all the villagers are avoiding me."

"Don't you know?"

I shook my head.

"Well, it's because the place is haunted."

"What?"

"Yes, it's because of what happened there." And then the man sat down to tell me the story of the gruesome murders that had taken place inside my home.

◆ ◆ ◆

He told me why my house had stayed empty for almost two years before I had moved in. His story explained why the foreman had been so reluctant to rent the place to me.

Before I had ever set my sights on this small village by the river, a husband and wife couple lived in the hut I now called my home. They had been married for some time and had lived in the village for several years. Although many people knew them, not everyone in town liked them. The wife was a simple, sympathetic woman, but her husband was another card altogether. Where she was kind and a little timid, he was domineering and a perpetual drunkard. He had broken his knee once while working in one of the fields of the farming villages nearby, and although he had recovered with only a slight limp, if anything so much as bothered him, he would moan on and on about his busted knee and would take to the bottle at the drop of a hat.

Needless to say, the old drunkard had had trouble maintaining a steady job. This put pressure on the wife, who often had to stay at home and make ends meet on her husband's fluctuating salary.

The wife tolerated her husband's behavior at first. Mostly because she understood the pain caused by the injury, and because of her husband's reactions. If she ever questioned or criticized his need to drink, the husband would take to beating her.

When their finances got bad and her husband's behavior worsened, the neighbors nearby would often hear the sound of shouting and of pots and pans flying around their thatched hut by the river. The husband would begin by cursing out his wife if she dared to criticize him. He would slap her if it got worse, and then he would threaten to kill her if things got even worse.

And things did. After spending almost three months without any steady work or steady pay, one day the wife decided to do something while her husband was out drinking rice wine in a field somewhere. She went to the local indigo dyeing plant and got herself a job in the factory. After working the whole day staining cloth, she came back home with the promise of a steady income to find her husband pacing restlessly in their hut. He was angry at her for coming back so late. He felt frustrated that the dinner had not been made on time. Moreover, he was suspicious.

"Where have you been?" he interrogated his wife, gripping her arm hard even as she tried to twist away.

His wife tried to explain to him how she had gotten a new job, how they would have more money and food now, how dinner would be ready in no time.

But her angry husband, already drunk on wine, would have none of it. He didn't care about his wife's new job, and he didn't care about her lousy reassurances. What he cared about was she was late, and he had a pounding headache, and his stomach growled with an uncontrollable hunger. He had to teach his disobedient wife a lesson, he thought in his stupor.

So he got what was closest to hand—a broomstick—and ran after his poor wife. But she, who was used to his antics, dodged the first couple of blows. She ran into the kitchen and picked up a large pan to use as a shield. Each time her husband tried to hit her, she countered his move like a seasoned duelist. Between the snap of wood on metal and metal on wood, the husband and the wife would trade insults. Her husband called her an ungrateful, cheating, lazy, loose woman, and the wife called her husband an aimless, deadbeat loser, and much worse. By the time his wife had called him the son of a donkey and thrown every insult possible at him, he had had enough. He reached behind his wife and grabbed a small machete she used to grind fresh coconut. Enraged beyond belief and unthinkingly, he took the knife and ran it across her throat to stop that insulting voice with one fatal sweep.

His wife's eyes bulged, and she completely stopped talking but not moaning as blood began to pool out in streams from her neck. She gave her husband a piercing cold glare before collapsing onto her knees. Her husband, shocked at the consequence of his own violence, fell forward too. He picked up his wife in his arms as she choked and then dragged her over to the small cot they shared.

His wife was losing blood, but her arms and legs still resisted him. She kept one hand in a painful grip on the gash across her neck and the other battled her stupid husband.

"Help! Help! Someone help me!" the foolish husband cried.

The whole neighborhood had heard the husband and wife arguing, and the violence of the commotion had drawn a crowd. Soon his neighbors were knocking on his door, threatening to tear it down. When the first neighbor came to knock down the couple's door, accusations of murder were already flying through the streets. The husband took one look at his wife's pale, stricken face and her sari covered in blood and knew he was done for.

Outside the neighbors counted to three before they barreled into the front door. In that moment, before the unwanted guests made their way through, the husband realized he had to save himself. He knew he couldn't survive if he was charged for the murder of his wife. So in a split second, he rushed into the kitchen, picked up the blood-stained machete, and plunged it into his heart.

And that's how the neighbors found them there—his wife dying, gasping for her last breath on the cot, and her husband bent over on the floor, dying as well.

◆ ◆ ◆

Having heard the strange, horrifying tale, I was momentarily speechless.

"But the foreman didn't tell me that a murder or even two had taken place in my house," I said.

"Who would tell you?" the man shook his head. "They would never be able to rent a house that way." Having told me the terrible story, he began to walk away in the direction of the miller's front gate.

"Wait. If there really were any murders in my house, how come the place was spotless and so neat and tidy when I moved in?"

"Think for a moment," he said with his hand on the latch. "Do you think anyone in the village would keep a small hut so neat and clean? No. After the murders, the villagers took away the mattress and the sheets. The foreman had the floor mopped and the walls re-painted. There's nothing in that house that indicates any violence occurred there. Well, except..." he trailed off.

"Except?"

"Except for the fact that it's haunted," he said with a dark grin. "The neighbors swear they can hear the sounds of pots and pans falling, bodies slumping to the floor, and mysterious moans from inside when the lights go out at night."

◆ ◆ ◆

"And was the place haunted?" I asked Tamal-da.

"Well," he said, turning his head to look out of the taxi and into the cloud-marked sky. "Let me tell you what happened later that night."

◆ ◆ ◆

I was always a bit of a heavy sleeper. I think it's because I had to wake up so early for work, and because I came home so late after dropping off my last customers in Kolkata. Sometimes I wouldn't even have time to cook dinner before I wandered into bed and fell asleep. I kept a pack of cigarettes on the kitchen windowsill, and on nights when I had nothing or no time to eat, I'd just smoke one before going to bed.

That evening after I had heard that odd story from the stranger, I made it a point to come home early. I skipped my last appointments of the night, claiming my stomach had started hurting after I had eaten some yellow-water puchkas at a local roadside stand. My fellow cabbies were sympathetic and my boss let me go home early. I drove home from Kolkata to the small village by the river in record time. I wanted to see what was going on.

I got home when the sun was just beginning to set on the horizon. It cast a fire-red glow over the river tracing my backyard. After watching the sun disappear, I retreated back into my house. The place almost looked unfamiliar as I walked in. The story was having an effect on me. But even as a child, I had never believed in ghosts or dark places.

So I made myself a cup of tea and a fried potato to have with leftover rock-hard roti. Having eaten a full and satisfying meal, I took out a cigarette to smoke as I washed the dishes in the sink. After dinner, I went to fetch more water from the pump. I saw some neighbors there, who as usual, refused to speak to me or even look my way.

"Don't worry," I said with the cigarette butt still dangling from my lips, "they don't exist."

Some of the neighborhood women gave me a nasty look before trotting off.

Back at home, I still had time before bed, so I first went around inspecting the cot, then the floor, and then the kitchen for any bloodstains. But everywhere I looked, I found nothing unusual. So after reading a week-old newspaper I had laying around, I finally decided to get some sleep. That man was crazy, I thought just before drifting off.

In truth, that night was just like any other. I slept comfortably with the windows open, the cool air creating a nice breeze in the room. I slept deeply and dreamt of my father taking me fishing for the first time, of our first time to the village Kali temple, of our first—

Boom!

In a moment, I sat upright in my bed. All of my memories of my childhood home had drifted from my mind and out the front door when I heard that god-awful noise!

Boom!

It happened again. It sounded like a loud but muffled thud as if a body were falling from a great height. And then a moment of silence. And then the sound of rustling, creeping steps.

What could that be? I thought, clutching my blanket. *Why was this happening to me on this night right after I had heard such a dreadful story?*

The wind was picking up through the trees. As I opened the front door, the night greeted me with a howl.

I walked around the perimeter of the house, half expecting to encounter a merry mischief-maker, or an unexpected ghost. But I didn't see anything. Outside of my own solitary footsteps, there was no sign of life. There was only the howling wind and the small village, slumbering and silver-lit under the moonlight.

The road and yard in front of my small house were completely empty, and the night was cold. I wished I had brought a kambal or something to keep me warm.

I looked towards the miller's house but saw no lights burning in his cottage. I thought perhaps a wild animal had come by, but there were no tracks at all in the dust and mud surrounding my house.

◆ ◆ ◆

"Do you really think it was a ghost?" I asked Tamal-da as a particularly violent gust of wind shook our stranded Ambassador cab. The rain was picking up now and the sky seemed darker. The three teenage boys, our would-be rescuers, were nowhere in sight. Aside from the rivers of water, the street was completely empty. It was as if Kolkata had become a ghost town in the rain.

"Well," Tamal-da said, resting his hand on the steering wheel, "you know I don't believe in ghosts, so I'll tell you what happened."

◆ ◆ ◆

For the next half hour or so, I continued to survey the interior and exterior of the house. The wind blew through in gusts, causing a shutter to move back and forth, and created a click-clacking sound, nothing like the loud boom and scurrying footsteps I had heard before. So I decided to take another walk around the house, and that's when I saw it.

On a huge pile of grain at the edge of the miller's yard and near the front corner of my house were two large coconuts. They had fallen a great height— from one of the towering palm trees that surrounded our houses and stood over the grains.

◆ ◆ ◆

"So that, didi," Tamal-da said, laughing, "was the truly mysterious and other-worldly ghost."

"Oh," I said and sat back on my heels. "I was expecting a real ghost story."

"Sorry, I told you I don't believe in ghosts."

"So your house isn't haunted?" I asked.

"Not in the least," Tamal-da took out a handkerchief to clean his glasses, then blew his nose before going on. "I never found a sign of ghosts there after that night. No funny sounds in the evening or strange stains around the house. Besides I don't believe in ghosts, so why would they bother me? I always pray to Ma Kali in the morning, and she has always protected me."

"Oh," I said, turning away from him and staring out the window. "It's just that I love a good ghost story."

"Hmm," he looked thoughtful for a moment. "Well, I didn't tell you about how I became such a devotee of Ma Kali, did I?"

"No," I replied.

"Well, it began in the village where I grew up. I can't say that what happened to me there was an encounter with a ghost or not. After all, I don't believe in such things. All I can say with any certainty, though, is whatever did happen to me there, I cannot explain it, even today."

"What happened?" I asked.

"Where should I begin?"

Kolkata, as you know, was not always my home. I moved to the city when I was fourteen, but I spent my childhood and youth growing up in a village many kilometers from here. I grew up near a place called Krishnapur, in the heart of West Bengal. My father was a fisherman by trade as was his father and his father before him. Our household was small. My grandparents had died when I was young, and my mother had had trouble conceiving a second child. So I grew up mostly alone in our small house in a village where many of my aunts, uncles, cousins, and distant relatives lived.

Our village bordered the outskirts of Krishnapur. There were many rice paddies on the land that belonged to our village. Almost everyone in the village knew, or had heard of, one another. In the late summer, when I was fourteen, an illicit love affair became the meal of the country gossip.

The local indigo dyer had a beautiful, young daughter named Lokhi. I remember that she had long, glossy black hair and eyes that shone as if the moon had been plucked out of the night's sky. I didn't know her personally, but sometimes I would come across her on the road, on the way to the water pump, or on the dirt path to the neighboring village.

The talk of that summer was how Lokhi had fallen in love with a merchant's son who lived in a village across the vast jungle that separated us. Lokhi must have been sixteen or seventeen at that time.

She had fallen in love brashly, and without remorse. Even though her father had planned to marry her off into another family who worked in textiles like he did, Lokhi would have none of it. She and the merchant's son would often meet secretly on the banks of the river at night or in the middle of the deep, dark jungle where no one would find them.

One day, news from the neighboring village came that the merchant had threatened to throw out his son from the house if he didn't stop his outlandish affair with Lokhi soon. The merchant's son was a few years older than her, and he, too, had been betrothed to marry a young woman from a merchant's family who was not as destitute, or as beautiful, as Lokhi.

Although Lokhi's father made a decent living, he was not in the social or financial ranks of the merchant and his family. Moreover, his daughter had stopped going to school as a young girl so she could help with her family's small dyeing station. A merchant's family that was well to do would never accept a poor, illiterate village girl as their daughter-in-law. No, the merchant's family was ambitious, and they had social goals.

These were the rumors and gossip flying back and forth between our village and the merchant's one, and in time, the stories even made their way to the street markets of Krishnapur.

One morning when I woke up to join my father, who had already left to go fishing with my uncle and cousins, my mother told me the latest gossip about Lokhi over our morning tiffin.

"Did you hear, Khoka," she said, crouched on the kitchen floor and frying a luchi with leftover oil for me, "Lokhi ran away yesterday."

"She did?" I asked between mouthfuls of luchi wrapped around the aloo-tarkari dish my mother had just made. We usually ate two meals together and my mother would always save the best portions—a bit of potato or a small piece of fish—for me to eat.

"Yes," she said, shaking her head as she flipped over the bread in the iron wok. "That crazy girl finally decided to elope with that merchant's no-good son. Who knows how they'll fare together, just two young kids without any money or family to support them." My mother gave me a steaming hot luchi before taking leftover bread to eat herself. "The merchant will probably come after them with a broom or even an arrest warrant," she chuckled, dipping into her food.

Sitting next to my mother on the cold mud floor, I thought about this for a moment before my imagination took off in the direction of fishing. It was almost half past three in the morning, or I should say deep in the night. I would be joining my father and cousins on the fishing boat in half an hour. Since I was the youngest of the crew, I was allowed to eat a quick breakfast before coming in later with the extra nets and tackles they would need. I was daydreaming about the kinds and amount of fish we could catch when my mother reminded me about the time.

"You had better hurry now or you'll be late," she said licking her hands clean.

I nodded and drank the water in the stainless steel cup. Washing my hands with the rest, I quietly grabbed the extra nets, finishing lines and tackles, and ran out the door.

"I'll see you later today, Ma!" I yelled towards her through the open kitchen door as I hurried towards the dirt path leading into the jungle. "I'll be home after the market closes in Krishnapur!"

"Don't be too late, Khoka," my mother waved, wiping a wet hand on her sari anchal, "and take care."

I waved back to her before taking off.

It was very early morning, an hour or two before dawn, so the jungle seemed dark and mysterious as I entered it. The bright, silvery beams cast down upon the jungle floor by the full moon above, lit my way. As I moved past an ancient banyan trees and high palms, the moon peaked through the dense foliage—playing a game of hide-and-seek with me. The night was unusually chilly, and I wrapped the netting around my thin t-shirt and short slacks to keep warm. My sandals slapped against the bottom of my feet as I hopped over rocks and tree roots. I heard the sounds of animals, owls hooting, crickets chirping, and the rustling caused by something else as I moved forward. From the corner of my eye, I saw a strange shape flit before me. It looked to be the figure of a woman, draped in a white sari and fleeing at an inhumanly rapid pace through the woods.

Seeing her with her dark hair flying wildly behind her, I tried to call out in the direction of the running figure, but she did not turn around. So I began to run too.

But the girl ran unusually fast. Even running at a marathon pace, as if I were running for my own life, I could not keep up with her.

By the time I reached the old Kali Mandir in the woods, I had lost sight of the shadowy white figure completely. Walking by the main gate to the temple, I stopped in front of the arched entrance way. The priest had not gotten up yet and had not opened the doors this early in the morning. But through the grilled gates, I could see into the main temple hall which rose majestically in the middle of the forest. Looking in, I saw the figure of Kali standing there, in the middle of the hall, with her wide and sinister grin. Her tongue was hanging out and, in her hands, she carried a variety of weapons, including a machete in one and a knot of severed heads in another. Across her lithe blue, naked body, a garland of skulls draped lightly across her breasts. A short chain-mail skirt with links in the shape of human hands hiked up one of her hips as she stood with her legs parted wide on the body of her husband, Shiva. Her tongue, thus, rolled down of its own accord. Bracketed against the moonlight, she made a ferocious figure. But there was something protective, even eternal about her too. There was an air of mischief in her smile and the way her body posed provocatively for the spectator. But in her eyes, there was something maternal, kind, and even graceful.

Watching the stationary figure watch me, I gave her a quick morning prayer. *Mother Kali, Kali of the night, please protect me and those I love. Dear Kali, full of grace.*

I said the prayer silently and then gave her a clasped hand pranam. In the moonlight, the statue's eyes glittered back at me.

I glanced back at the statue one last time before heading in the direction of the river. I was passing by the dirt path that led to the neighboring village when I noticed a strange movement. It was that woman in the white sari. Like before, she was moving abnormally fast, ducking behind and in front of trees at an unusual rate.

At last, I followed her into a small clearing where I felt something tap hard against my head. I backed up, looking to see if I had run into a branch, or if someone had thrown a stone at me.

Moving back, I almost screamed when I saw what it was. A foot was dangling at my shoulder height. I closed my eyes, hoping it was just an apparition.

But when I opened them again, I realized it was a real foot, made of flesh and blood, hanging before me. And unfortunately the foot was attached to a small, slender body gently swaying in the breeze, shrouded by moonlight and foliage in the middle of the vast jungle.

It was a young woman with long, flowing hair. She hung by a rope on a tall tree branch. She wore a pale colored sari with paisleys on it, and her flying hair obscured her face. Her forehead had a small trace of vermilion on it, and on her dangling wrists were red and white Sadiel bracelets that looked cracked and badly broken. Her hands and feet had been painted with mehndi and glowed a garish red in the moonlight.

I did not have to see her face to know who she was. This was Lokhi's body swaying before me, still dressed in the costume of a bride in a pale pink sari with pretty red designs on it, she looked as if she should be celebrating her wedding night rather than hanging from this tree.

Had she done this to herself? I thought, steading my nerves as I reached out to touch her foot. Her leg was cold to the touch. Although her body swayed slightly, she didn't appear to be moving of her own volition. By all appearances, it looked like she had died several hours ago.

But the broken bangles left an unsettled feeling in my stomach. *How could such a slight girl climb such a large tree and do this to herself?* I looked up at the tall tree branch which was a good meter and a half above my head.

Shaking my head slightly, I closed my eyes, but I couldn't get the afterimage of her forlorn, looming figure out of my mind. So after a moment of hesitation, I dropped my netting and fishing wares and went yelling out of the jungle and straight back to my home village.

"Help! Help! Somebody help!" I shouted as loud as I could. As I crossed Kali temple, the lights inside began to flicker on. But I needed more than an old priest to help me, so I ran through the jungle screaming like a banshee until I got home.

By the time I reached my front door step, my mother, uncle, and quite a few neighbors had arrived.

"It's Lokhi," I said, and tried to retell the story of how I had found her in the middle of the woods. Hearing my frantic words, many of the village elders ordered a search party to be formed, and we left for the jungle with torches and knives in our hands.

I led the way with my uncle beside me—my mother staying back and praying for our safe return. As the sun had not risen yet, it was still hard to navigate the jungle, especially with such a large group, but we soon made our way over.

When I saw the clearing up ahead, I ran to the spot where I had found Lokhi hanging. I half expected her body to have disappeared. I wanted it all to be a bad dream, a nightmare from which I could awake.

But when I got to the clearing, I realized I hadn't made a mistake. The beautiful girl was still dangling there in her makeshift wedding sari. Still virginal, and still very dead.

One of the villagers ran up to check her pulse and then jumped up to see if she had any breath. After a moment, he shook his head slowly. The bleak look in his eyes said it all.

"We should cut her down," someone else said. A chorus of agreement followed.

"You should go," someone from the back pushed me forward, shoving a knife into my hand.

"Because you're the smallest and the lightest, it would be faster if you climbed the tree than us."

I looked up at the stony expression of the man who had handed me the knife. *I was the only child in the group of men. What could I say to them?*

I scrambled up the tree, my nails digging into the ancient bark. Once up, I lightly walked onto the branch. It felt like a tightrope act—too risky, too dangerous. So I sat down and slowly slid myself forward. With the knife clasped in my mouth, I used my hands to pull myself towards the thick hanging rope.

The rope was double-knotted. From the branch, I could see Lokhi's beautiful head. What did her face look like, I wondered, imagining her lovely eyes glazed over in death. It was a macabre thought, but it was the only thing that raced through my mind as I spent those few excruciating minutes cutting her free from the rope. A few men below caught her body as she fell.

"We have to perform funeral rites," someone down below suggested.

"Yes, let's get her to the creek at the back of our village," someone else said.

"Wait, wait!" I shouted, still sitting on the branch. "What about telling her family? What about telling the police? This could have been a murder!"

"What murder?" an old white-haired man replied. "Who would murder such a stupid girl? No, she did this to herself when she realized the merchant's son would never marry her. If we get the police involved, they'll only cause more trouble for both her family and for us. Why create a larger mess?"

"But—" I said, trying to scramble down from the branch. As I reached the trunk, a young man stepped forward.

"I'm her cousin," he said, "I'll take care of her." He took her body in his embrace, and the remaining villagers followed him out into the night. The priest was not even with them, so where and how they did the funeral rites, I'll never know. All I know is that Lokhi's body was cremated and her ashes scattered. I know that the police never came to our village, and neither did the merchant's family.

Climbing down from the tree, silence greeted me. My uncle stood below and placed a hand on my shoulder. We did not say anything to each other but gathered up our fallen fishing nets and tackles and went home, walking in silence that day.

◆ ◆ ◆

After that day, things resumed as they had always been in the village. Each morning, two hours before dawn, I would get up to have an early breakfast with my mother before joining my father, uncle, and cousins on the fishing boats.

Two days after Lokhi's death and funeral, I had gone through the dark jungle to resume fishing on the river. Many of the villagers in town hadn't dared to enter the jungle after dark and sometimes even during the day. They feared that Lokhi's spirit, which had not been granted a proper funeral and which had been taken from life so unexpectedly, still roamed the night and settled under trees, awaiting its next victim.

I, of course, did not believe in ghosts, so I saw these stories as mostly hogwash. My family had to make a living, and I had to work to do my part for them. I could not sit at home and cower in the dark and fear entering the jungle because of the rumors of her ghost or her possible murderers roaming the night there. No, there was no time for such idle or fantastical speculation.

When I reached the river that ran past the jungle, my father and uncle would already have the canoes set up for fishing. My cousins would hoist the nets onto the boat and then we would take off in the dark water hoping to get a good catch of fish. About a half hour later, I would take the first large net, filled with the catch of the day, back through the jungle and towards the morning market in Krishnapur.

Once I resumed fishing, the routine went on like this day after day. A few weeks after Lokhi's death, the gossip and speculation over her suicide were beginning to die down in the village. Her mother and father still looked forlorn, but her younger siblings would often be seen playing outside and smiling in the dirt paths. Slowly but surely, life regained its old monotony. Family and monetary feuds continued to be the main point of debate and conflict in the village, and my training as a fisherman continued as before. Almost a month later, people were beginning to break the taboo of entering the jungle at night. Everything once again became comfortable and mundane. Old stories and old fears were once again forgotten.

One morning I went to work as usual after my early morning meal with my mother. The full moon was out and I was whistling a cheerful tune. There was a new cinema coming to Krishnapur, and I had already heard some of the pop songs from the film which played on the radio at the stall next to ours in Krishnapur.

This day the wind was heavy and the gusts carried my song out into the jungle. Other than the whispering wind, no sounds greeted me in the dark woods. It appeared that all the animals, even the nocturnal ones, had gone to sleep for the night, or perhaps they were just waiting for something.

Shaking my heard at the fanciful thought, I followed the dirt trail that led to the river via the Kali temple. The fishnets and tackle itched against my back. Adjusting them, I walked deeper into the woods.

A good one hundred meters or so into the forest, I noticed the first unusual sighting of the night. Some meters ahead of me, in the shade between two trees, a spark ignited and then burst into flame.

What was that, I wondered, going completely still. The small ball of fire crackled like a sparkler and changed color from a low blue-green to a deep red-orange before going out. In a split second, the fire, which had been burning so brightly, vanished into the night.

Shaking my head with disbelief, I walked to the spot where I had seen it. There were no signs of matches, fireworks, or even footsteps in the wet mud where I had seen the fire alight. All of it was very strange.

Disgruntled, I began to turn back towards the river path when I saw another flame burst out of the corner of my eye. The flame sparked and transformed, changing shades as a bright, round orb. The orb of light was too small and too symmetrical to be caused by a torch, and the edges of the flame sparkled like a firecracker although the light was not caused by one.

Once again as the flame burnt, I tried to chase it, but once again, it went out before I reached it.

By the time I had reached the Kali Temple, I thought I saw the flame light again from a great distance, but when I spun around to find it, it was gone.

Walking close to the Kali Mandir gate, I offered the goddess a quick but respectful prayer as I did each morning before work. Looking at the statue's face, Kali's lips shone red, as did her long tongue in contrast with her bright white teeth and dark glittering eyes. In the moonlight, she seemed almost alive and even human that morning.

My imagination is running wild, I thought as I made myself trudge along the path towards the river. Finally reaching the banks, my father, uncle, and cousins had set up the two boats as usual. One of my cousins had already caught a big fish. And my father waited for me on shore and secured the extra nets on board before we embarked onto the water.

A half hour later, I took the first net full of fish back through the dark jungle. My cousin who had gotten the catch of the day had asked me to be careful with his big fish.

"Get a good price for it at the market," he had said to me.

I nodded and placed the heavy net bag on my back. Like before, the rope ties itched on my shoulder. I tried to adjust the jute and plastic straps as I moved through the dark woods. In doing so, I almost missed the spark of mysterious color-changing light. When I saw the place from which it had extinguished, I ran towards it, heavy bag and all.

Once I got to the place, the light burst into flame again at a far greater distance. How was it moving so fast in the woods, I thought as I ran at top speed after it.

The light would spark and flame out in all random directions. It looked to be switching-back through the woods at an inhuman pace, bursting into flames at faster intervals than before.

My breath became shallow and rapid as I ran behind it through the woods. Only when I reached the moonlit clearing between two trees did I realize where I was.

"Oh my god!" I muttered as I recognized the tall tree to the right. I tried to back away but managed to back up into the middle of the two trees, to the exact same spot where I—

Bam!

I felt a heavy weight come into contact with my forehead. It felt like the kick of a football player hitting me with full force as if my head were a mere ball and this was his only chance to make a field goal.

I could feel the indentation of small toenails scratching into the skin of my forehead as I fell backwards. My arms flailed and my legs lost their balance as I toppled over. I tried to keep my eyes open, but my head was spinning.

With an undignified thump, I landed backwards on top of the large netted bag full of fresh caught fish, the ropes of the bag tangled behind me, and the drawstring tied in a double knot around my right wrist bit into my skin as I fell down.

In the last moments before losing consciousness, I saw the full moon glaring down at me above the branch of the tall tree where I had found Lokhi's body swinging.

There was no one and nothing in sight. Who could have kicked me from that height, I thought as my head pounded violently and the sound of my own breath roared through my ears. As my eyes closed of their own volition, I knew without a doubt I was the only human being in the entire jungle that night. As darkness overcame me, I had a vision of gleaming red-ochre eyes framed by long dark hair and a menacing smile full of white teeth.

"Ma Kali, help me," I whispered with my last breath before fainting into a dead black.

◆ ◆ ◆

Many hours later, I woke up to face a bright and glaring midday sun. A pair of hands moved my head from side to side.

"What happened?" someone asked.

"I don't know," another voice replied.

"Should we call a doctor?"

"Just wait a moment. It looks like the boy is coming to."

Blinking my eyes, I tried to use my left hand to block out the vision of the super-nova white sun.

"Ow," I said, struggling to sit upright but falling back again. Every part of my body hurt, including my head which throbbed as if a bomb had detonated inside of it.

"Are you okay?" a voice asked as a face came into view blocking the direct sunlight.

It was the old priest who worked at the Kali Mandir. His face was dry and gaunt from years of asceticism. His bushy, white eyebrows twitched over wire-rimmed glasses as he surveyed my face. His thin brown hands rotated my head slowly.

"Does that hurt?" he asked.

"A little," I replied.

"Manu, give me some water for this boy."

Manu, the priest's assistant who was in training, himself, came towards me with a small tin flask. He was a portly man of middle age with a big black moustache which spoke of the hair he must have had in his non-balding years.

He came smiling up at me and offered the open flask to my lips. I took a small sip at first and then I drank deeper, trying to get the desert-feel out of my mouth.

"Do you remember what happened to you?" the priest asked with a soothing voice.

"A little." I nodded, and rising up on one elbow, I told them about the strange night, the mysterious lights I had seen in the jungle, how I had chased after them and had ended up being kicked in the forehead under Lokhi's tree.

"Are you sure those odd lights weren't torches, and the kick you felt was not something you had run into, or a stone or a stick thrown your way?"

"No, the lights sparkled and changed color," I said. "They were too small to be torches and too full of flame to be proper fireworks. "And it definitely was not a branch that hit me." I shook my head. "I was standing in this clearing under these two large trees where Lokhi was hung. There were no other sticks and branches to get in my way. It felt like flesh and bone coming into contact with my forehead. I even felt the sting of toenails digging into me."

"Hmm," the priest murmured and again turned my head this way and that.

"Oh, God!" Manu exclaimed and pointed at my forehead with a shaking finger. "The ghost of Lokhi has come after him!"

"Be quiet, Manu," the priest dismissed his overacting assistant and turned to me. "You said you were coming back from fishing when the incident happened?"

"Yes, I was going to sell our first morning catch in Krishnapur. If I only had stayed on the path, I would be there right now and not lying in the dirt in broad daylight," I said, my breath picking up speed.

"But if you had gone fishing," the priest said slowly, "where in god's name, are your fish?"

"My fish?" I asked, surprised. I remembered the overwhelming smell of recently caught fish as I had collapsed, fainting onto the net in the moonlight after someone had kicked me.

"Why," I said, "they're in the bag behind me." I sat up quickly, noting the large portion of the net bag stuck under my bum. Turning on my side, I pointed to the rest of the netted bag which I had fallen on.

I expected to see a whole pile of rotten fish creating a putrid stench in the mid-afternoon sun. But instead an empty bag greeted me.

"What!" I exclaimed in surprise. My body had landed soundly on the fish. The plastic and jute ropes which secured the bag were still tied in a double knot on my right wrist.

I scrambled to my feet and pulled the net-bag up with my right hand.

"I don't believe this," I said. There was no sign of fish anywhere. But more disturbingly, there was no sign of force either. The ropes wrapped around my wrist had not been tampered with. They were knotted exactly as I had left them, and there were no knife cuts or slash marks on the body of the bag either. No one had tried to steal the fish by ripping the bag open.

"My cousin's fish!" I said miserably as I surveyed the empty bag, wishing the fish to magically reappear.

"Your cousin's fish?" the priest asked.

"Yes, my cousin caught a prize fish today. It was so large and tasty looking. He had asked me to sell it at a good price in the morning market of Krishnapur, and I promised I would make a good profit off of it. Oh, god, he's going to kill me when he finds out I lost his fish!"

"Hmm," the priest rubbed his chin and looked thoughtful. He looked like he was going to offer me advice as he rearranged his shawl across his boney shoulders, but then Manu interrupted.

"Do you know what that means?" he said, sticking his round, baby face into mine.

"That I'm in a lot of trouble?"

"No. It means you survived Lokhi's attack because of the fish."

"What!" I said, folding my hands on my hips.

"Yes, yes," Manu chatted. "Yes, on the one month anniversary of Lokhi's death you were lured into the jungle by her ghost. The strange lights were a way of entrancing you. When you first entered the forest, you did not follow their trail all the way. But on the way back from fishing, Lokhi knew this was her only chance to exact her revenge on you. She was angry at you for the way you had revealed her dead body to the villagers and for cutting her down so her body could be cremated before any real investigation was performed. She haunts this place as the villagers say. And on the night of the full moon, she waited here for you and lured you here so she could finally attack!"

"Attack? But other than a pounding headache and sore aching bones, I'm quite alright."

"Exactly!" Manu exclaimed with a gleam in his eyes. "You are fine because of the fish. Everyone knows a Bengali spirit has a particular soft spot for fish. When Lokhi got a sniff of the recently killed animals, she couldn't resist. So instead of devouring you whole, she devoured the fish."

I stared at Manu as he nodded sagely.

"Don't scare the boy," the priest muttered as he picked up his satchel and placed the flask inside.

"Yes, yes," Manu patted my shoulder, and he went on as if expecting another reprimand from his boss.

"That is probably why you survived," he whispered into my ear as we followed the priest who was already walking in the direction of the Kali temple. The priest waited a meter or two ahead of us so we could catch up with him.

As we walked up to the old man, Manu asked hurriedly, "Did you say anything to Lokhi's ghost when you saw her?"

"Well, first of all," I said, nudging him in the ribs, "I don't believe in ghosts, so whatever happened to me, it could not have been Lokhi's spirit because how could her ghost really exist?" I shook my head in Manu's direction as he looked back at me with pleading eyes.

"Plus," I continued just as we reached the priest, "I didn't say anything to Lokhi's ghost before I passed out. I just remember mumbling, 'Oh, Ma Kali,' and that's all."

"So you called to Kali," the old priest looked at me with soft eyes.

"Yes."

"Well, that's how you—" Manu began but was cut off.

"That's enough, Manu!" the priest reprimanded. "Let's take the poor boy home."

◆ ◆ ◆

Tamal-da's story ended as we spotted the figures of the three teenage boys running our way. Behind them came a ragged older man pulling a beat-up rickshaw. The old rickshaw was certainly no taxi, but it had wheels and could move and take us to a place where we could find more help and transportation.

"Hey look," I said, pointing from the backseat. "The boys are back." The rain had stopped falling so heavily now, and a light drizzle pervaded the sky. The street, though still flooded, looked less impassable as the water had drained to ankle height.

"Let me go call them," Tamal-da said, reaching out to open his driver's side door.

"Wait," I said, resting a hand on his shoulder. "Did you ever figure out what really happened to you that night?"

"No," he shook his head ruefully as he looked back at me. "I never did."

"You don't believe it was really her ghost, do you?"

"Well," he said after a pause, "that I cannot say. All I know is that the villagers decided the jungle was doubly haunted after my incident with the fish."

"And what did you decide?" I asked.

"I decided after that day that fishing was not the best career choice for me. So first I quit fishing and then I quit the village altogether. I then moved to Kolkata and became a taxi driver. I never went back to the jungle at night, and I haven't been back home ever since."

"But doesn't your family miss you?" I asked.

"They do," he nodded, "a little. I try to make enough money so my parents can come visit me during the puja season. They often bring prasads from home."

"That's sweet." I smiled, and with a mischievous grin, I tried one last time to get the truth out of him. "So you really don't believe in ghosts?" I asked as he hopped out of the car and into the wet street.

He closed the door tightly and then poked his head in through the open window.

"All I can say is I've been a devoted follower of Kali since that day." And with a smile, he took off to greet our would-be rescuers.

BRAVE ENOUGH TO FOLLOW

Megan Steusloff

IT BEGAN WITH A GIRL named Sadie Thompson. She was born during the night of a horrible thunderstorm raging over the plantation owned by her father. According to the stories, Sadie's mother reminded her every day of the terrible pain she had caused her that night. A midwife cleaned and checked her over and handed Sadie first to her mother and finally her father. He felt so disappointed that she was not a boy, he left as soon as the storm broke and did not come back for five months, claiming he was off to important business in Charleston. When guests or relatives visited the plantation, Sadie's mother displayed her token child, but Sadie was primarily cared for by the servants.

On the plantation, she lived a life of distinct isolation. Sadie began crawling to the slave cabins as soon as she was strong enough to do so. Her mother either did not notice or did not care, so the child kept crawling back there as often as she could. It was common for young children of plantation owners to show interest in slave children, and for Sadie it was the best way to spend her time. Her earliest memories were of spinning and swaying in a lovely summer breeze, listening to songs and clapping and praying and chanting and stories told in a mixture of English and the Gullah language. Her father, Jacob, claimed their slaves were wild animals that should be ignored and avoided. But to Sadie, many of the slaves became her friends.

Jacob saw his slave, Mama Fato, as pure money. An "excellent breeder" who had eight healthy, living children, Mama Fato had no trouble getting or staying pregnant, and the ability to work hard even with a blossoming belly and tiny mouths to feed. In return, Jacob allowed her and her husband to remain on the plantation without fear of being separated or sold. Not that he would have considered getting rid of Papa Vandi anyway. A rough and powerful driver in the rice fields, Papa Vandi kept each slave in place and working hard. Jacob would threaten to bring in a strict white overseer, but Papa Vandi led the slaves. His aggressiveness and strength filled everyone with fear, including Sadie.

Taken from the "Rice Coast" of Sierra Leone due to the strength, skills and knowledge he held, Papa Vandi was sold at a much higher bid than other impending slaves to Jacob Thompson. Although Jacob often mentioned the price he paid for Papa Vandi at auction, he had no regrets about this purchase. Under Papa Vandi's leadership, the rice crops produced consistent and impressive profits. Besides, Sadie's father spent almost all of the growing season in Charleston to avoid the yellow fever and malaria that brewed to life in the rice fields, leaving his wife to run the plantation, Papa Vandi to control the fields, and Sadie to do as she pleased between them.

For many years, the crops were prosperous and the slaves worked hard and seemed obedient. Sadie grew happily near the children of Mama Fato and Papa Vandi. She recognized the difference between herself and her friends, but, out of her mother's sight, Sadie's fair skin and light eyes clapped and hugged and intertwined with their soft, dark features. She snuck them leftover beef and fish, eggs, and sugar, in addition to soap, ribbons for their hair, and scraps of material for mending holes in their clothes.

The children of Mama Fato and Papa Vandi—Isaiah, the twins Seba and Saul, Juba, Tucker, Kizzy, Hannah, and the baby Pheby—were the first to receive Sadie's gifts and treasures. As time went on, she became friends with many of the slave children. There were a few young children living in family units; toddler brothers Kaapo and Jabari living with their grandmother, and twelve-year-old Tadeo and his seven-year-old sister, Louisa, living with their mom. Other children on the plantation had been separated from their families at the auctions, and Jacob had purchased them in preparation for the future. Three girls ranging between eight and ten years old, Fanny, Luzinka, and Malindi, had developed a sisterly affection for each other as they were taught their domestic duties around the big house, while two boys, Axum and Maceo, both presumed to be around fourteen, looked out for each other in the fields.

From her friends, Sadie learned about farming rice along with other crops. She learned about the weather and the stars. She learned about God and about love. Sadie secretly followed them to their Sunday services out on the far edges of the plantation, clapping to their songs and listening to the stories of times long ago, of sacrifice and discipleship, of salvation and resurrection. Bible stories passed down without the Bible to hold. The adults who spoke out and lifted up their voices at the services were emotional and passionate, sharing the hopes and dreams of generations before them, and letting them echo and resonate through the countryside.

Sadie taught her friends letters, reading, and writing. She read and spoke of places where there were no slaves. She started with Tucker, Kizzy, Hannah, Kaapo, Jabari, and Louisa, the very young slaves who were not as missed or sought after during the day. Most lessons were short and simple in the dirt; numbers, letters, names, and common words. Sometimes she would share her books to show photographs and illustrations of places real and make–believe. Whenever she could, she shared with the older children, and even the adults, after the Sunday service had concluded and they all mulled around enjoying the brief break. The stories were the real bond between Sadie and the slaves: their stories about clever animals and eternal hope; her stories about freedom and justice.

Sadie's favorite story Mama Fato told was about a very bossy elephant. The elephant had many animal friends, including a hippopotamus, monkey, tiger, and giraffe. One day, the friends wanted to play together, but whenever anyone suggested a game, the bossy elephant would say it was no fun and refuse to take part. Finally, they all asked elephant to choose what to do, and because he was so big and smart, he suggested they all just follow him. Elephant was constantly reminding his friends that he was the best leader, and they should listen to him and do what he did. As he was bossing his friends, he forgot to look where he was going, and the elephant got his head stuck in a twisted branch of an enormous tree. His friends saw what happened, stared at him for a moment, and walked away. The wise old lion watching from afar approached elephant and explained that true leaders listen, see the beauty and worth in others, and allow others to shine. Then he helped elephant get out of the twisted branch, bowed politely, and was off. From that day forward, elephant was the leader he was meant to be, and brought out the best in all of his friends.

Sadie's favorite story to tell the slaves was about Thomas Jefferson and his belief that everyone deserved personal liberty. She had been given a book on the founding fathers for her birthday and instantly took a liking to Jefferson, his writing style, his hopes for the new nation, and most of all, his view that slavery was against the laws of nature. While her parents thought she was learning dates and facts about honorable men of history, Sadie was actually beginning to discover she was not the only one who felt slavery was wrong. She began to secretly share these writings with the slaves on her father's plantation.

For all the coldness she received from her mother, Sadie found warmth and acceptance in the shack of Mama Fato. For all the anguish and fear the slaves felt toward her father, their master, and the whites who bought and sold humans as if they were animals, Papa Vandi, Mama Fato, their children, and many of the other slaves allowed Sadie into their homes and hearts. Each night, as darkness fell, Mama Fato would wait for Sadie to come before beginning to tell her stories. Papa Vandi would nod at her from the fields and, if no one was watching, allow her to tag along. Many of the slaves on the Thompson plantation saw something unique in Sadie.

Sadie loved to learn, understand and discover, and so did Mama Fato and her children. Despite the danger, she smuggled her friends books like *Pretty Little Stories for Pretty Little People*. While working with Sadie, Mama Fato and the children quickly gained knowledge and skills. Her friend's surreptitious letter formation led to words, sentences, and ideas worth writing down. Number recognition led to number sense. Over time, Sadie shared the understanding of the value of currency and coins. Sadie did not want any one of the slaves to be taken advantage of when they gained the freedom to sell their own wares like free blacks in the north.

One Sunday afternoon, a preacher visited the plantation and Sadie's mother invited him to dinner. Sitting silently at the elegant dining table, twelve-year-old Sadie listened to the preacher describe a man by the name of Frederick Douglass to her parents.

"He somehow learned how to read and write behind his master's back. He got caught trying to escape once and was sent to the fields under the slave breaker by the name of Covey. Then one day, he was gone. In a correspondence from my brother-in-law, I learned that this Douglass recently spoke at a convention in Seneca Falls. A slave orator trying to end slavery and give women rights. I tell you the world is changing. I don't like it one bit. There is a place for slaves in the fields and for women in the home, and that is how God intended it to be." Butter smeared his lips and breadcrumbs hung on his tangled beard as the preacher spoke, but Sadie watched him in fascination, as if he were the most beautiful man in the world.

Sitting tall, proud, and proper at the table, and having yet to touch her food, Sadie's mother responded, "That is absurd. What could an escaped slave possibly have to say that is worth listening to?"

"Absolutely nothing to be sure. This Douglass is ridiculous. The world is, and will remain, as it should be. As God intended," Sadie's father said.

They laughed at the thought of a slave writer and teacher. All they could think about was never letting slaves on this plantation come up with such a notion. Slaves must know their place or else pay the consequences.

Jacob looked at Sadie with contempt and said, "This information does not leave this table. Do you understand?"

Sadie nodded. Moments later, she asked to be excused. As she exited the room, the conversation turned to her father laughing about how odd she was, and how she actually enjoyed walking the fields and watching the slaves at work. Perhaps they had spoiled her with freedom.

"She is lucky to be so pretty because no gentleman in the world would ever understand her peculiar mindset and interests."

A few hours later, she snuck out her usual way, through the servant named Ellie's quarters and backdoor. Ellie squeezed her hand as she walked by. It was already late, and most of the slaves were sleeping. Sadie went straight to her haven, the shack of Papa Vandi and Mama Fato and their children. She stood outside the open door and whispered, "Papa, Mama, I have news. Amazing news."

The enormous man stooped through the doorway, followed closely by his wife. They both sat on the dirt next to Sadie. Their eyes ached with tiredness. He asked softly, "What is it, Miss Sadie?"

"Papa and Mama, the preacher says there is a man named Douglass. He was a slave. Now he is free. He is up north writing books and teaching about slavery. He is smart and brave. He's just like the both of you."

Papa and Mama sat for a long while next to Sadie, letting her words sink in. Mama wrapped the girl in her arms and rocked her gently. Papa hesitated to touch her, but after glancing around and seeing they were alone, he patted the top of her head and said, "Amazing news. Goodnight, Miss Sadie."

They stood and entered the dark shack behind them, leaving Sadie grinning on the stoop. Her own father and mother rarely touched her. To be given such affection by Mam Fato and Papa Vandi, well, that was almost as wonderful as hearing about Frederick Douglass.

Isaiah, the eldest child of Papa Vandi and Mama Fato, was a mere month older then Sadie. Free spirits, Isaiah and Sadie got on grandly together. Isaiah and Sadie grew up worlds apart, yet in each other's pockets. They shared endless whispered conversations and secret adventures. They appreciated the beauty of the land and explored every treasure it held together. When he wasn't working in the fields, Isaiah climbed trees and snuck off to catch crayfish with Sadie. After Sadie completed her studies and practiced on the piano, she would steal away to stroll through the meadows and splash in the lowlands with her pal.

Risky and rare, this type of friendship could only be understood by a few people closest to them. A white daughter of a plantation owner and a slave in the fields were not supposed to speak to each other with the exception of giving orders. Yet they wished on stars together every night she could get to the shack. They wished for the chance and ability to run away and leave her father's plantation behind. Sadie had big dreams, but little knowledge of how dangerous and improbable it was for slaves from the low country to escape and find freedom.

Sadie wanted all of her father's slaves to one day escape and find freedom, or be granted the right to work as paid laborers, but none more than her Izzy. As time went on and Sadie and Isaiah grew into young adults, their feelings for each other and their desire to run away grew as well. Sadie was confident her own parents were completely oblivious to how and where and with whom she spent her time. Sadie believed, however, that Mama Fato and Papa Vandi were always watching and knew both her and Isaiah much too well not be concerned.

She found herself walking the fine line between what was right and proper, and what her feelings and impulses pushed her to do. Time spent with Isaiah might be dangerous, but it was too wonderful to not take the risk.

By the time they turned fifteen years old, plans became more specific. They whispered about the best time of year and time of day to run, how many people they could logically bring with them without creating a huge stir, and how to get as far away as possible without anyone even noticing they were gone. Sadie studied and snuck maps to Isaiah. She also shared stories of trails and open-minded people she had heard about from guests on the plantation, and from reading her father's correspondences with other plantation owners. Masters shared ideas with her father of where to look for, and capture, runaway slaves, keeping everyone apprised of what could turn into a rebellion if not dealt with firmly and immediately.

For Sadie, it was the beginning of what could be a miracle for her, Izzy, and as many of the Papa Vandi and Mama Fato family they could realistically manage. Mama, Tucker, Juba, and the twins. Pheby could be carried the whole journey, Isaiah had insisted, so they had to take her. Sadie prayed for guidance and answers.

Jacob Thompson was home on the plantation during the winter and spring, but for the rainy summers and damp autumn months, he would find sanctuary in Charleston. Sadie always wondered about his lack of concern for his wife and daughter catching diseases, but was glad to see him go. When he was home, Sadie became the daughter she was expected to be. She sat on the veranda sipping iced tea, she entertained guests with her piano playing and beautiful singing voice, and she spent the long afternoons crocheting, oil painting, and reading scriptures.

It was challenging to escape her father's dictatorship, but she would sneak out every night she could manage for the stories of Mama Fato, with only the protective Ellie, the servant, and the vigilant eyes of Papa Vandi knowing where she had gone. She longed for her father to leave and wished the days away until early May.

The year Sadie turned seventeen, May came and went, but Jacob did not make the preparations to leave. It was not until Ellie, who possessed the best sewing skills on the plantation, was given all the materials for a dress that Sadie realized what was happening. A debutante ball. Her father was getting ready to give her away.

She cried to her mother, "How can he do this?"

"Well, what do you expect? You are a woman now," her mother responded.

Sadie crawled into the arms of Mama Fato, who rocked her gently, smoothing down her light brown hair, and whispered, "You must trust that all will be as it should. This is the path you must be brave enough to follow."

A few days after she was fitted for her gown, Sadie and Isaiah sat barefoot together in the creek. They watched the water flow over their skin and the tiny droplets sparkle in the sunshine. It was late afternoon on a Sunday, and the sun was still high in the heavens. After a few moments of sitting in silence, breathing in the beauty around them, they rose and began walking along the shore. Suddenly, Sadie slipped on a wet stone, and in her fall, gashed her lower leg on a jagged magnolia root. Blood raged into the water. She caught her breath.

Isaiah ripped off his shirt and tied it tightly around the wound. He lifted Sadie into his arms and raced to the big house. Jacob was on the porch with a visiting neighbor, smoking a pipe.

"Put her down, you beast. What did you do to her?" He backhanded Isaiah across the face without waiting for an answer.

"Papa, no! I fell at the creek! Stop!"

Her mother and servants came out in response to the commotion and swooped Sadie up and into the house.

Jacob grabbed Isaiah and tied his wrists around the nearest tree. Out came his whip. Sweat poured from Jacob as he swung the whip with all his might, splitting skin and spewing blood with every crack. Tears rolled down the face of Isaiah. Uncontrollable grunts of pain escaped from his mouth. Papa Vandi was close enough to witness his boy getting whipped. When Jacob saw him he ordered with fury, "Hey, Vandi, come and teach your poor excuse for a son here to not touch my daughter, to not look at my daughter, and to never set foot near this house again."

With a slow hand and a desperate apology, Papa Vandi took up the whip and began to beat his own son.

"It's okay, Pa. I'll be okay," Isaiah whispered, beginning to lose consciousness.

It was a week before Sadie could find a way to see him. She found him lying under a weeping willow, allowing the drooping fingers to tickle his arms and face without brushing them away. The summer sun was hanging low in the distance, and a chorus of insects sang all around.

"I am so sorry, Izzy," Sadie mumbled, crawling next to him and reaching to touch his arm. Her leg had been delicately wrapped in a sterile bandage, while the hardening and scabbing wounds covering Isaiah's back were raw against his filthy shirt.

"Stay away from me, girl. We can't be friends no more. I am a slave and you not. We can't go on anymore," Isaiah whispered in a flat, emotionless tone. He lay like a statue for a long moment then said in a much louder voice, "Go back home. Leave me be."

"You can't mean that! Just because of their ignorance. I'm that easy to dismiss? I am so sorry, Izzy." Sadie was shaking, sweat glistening on her forehead as she stood, walking backwards. Then she turned on her heel and ran, not towards the big house but towards the shacks that stood beside it.

As the sun melted into the horizon, Sadie found herself sitting at the edge of the creek beyond the slave shacks, meters away from where she had fallen. Isaiah was a tornado in her head. She considered what they each had said, and what she should have said. They had fought many times before, but he had never sounded so distant or indifferent. He did not follow her or call out for her. He wanted her gone. That realization haunted her more than the debutante ball approaching. Lost in her own thoughts, Sadie watched the water bubble and bounce over stones in the creek until distant drums startled her out of her reverie.

The ceremony started with a drumbeat to inform everyone that someone has died. Sadie rose and solemnly listened for the drumming to grow closer and pass by her as she courteously bowed her head. She followed behind the funeral party, always keeping a safe distance, to the sacred place set aside as a cemetery on the far eastern land of the plantation. She watched as the elders asked the ancestors for permission to enter. Amidst dancing, singing, and praying, the body of a young boy named Tadeo was wrapped in a cloth bag and lowered into the ground. Singing rang through the air as Isaiah assisted in shoveling damp earth over the corpse. Sadie wanted to join in the song, but knew it was not her place. A few meager dishes and bottles that could be spared were thrown and broken so no else would die soon. The children stood nearby grasping candles as the world around them grew dark. The women fashioned a grave marker with stones, shells, and small pieces of wood, and then the procession returned to the shacks. Over the next few hours, a saraka, or cooking ceremony, provided a feast to honor and celebrate the short life of Tadeo. Sadie listened to stories about his tendencies to catch bullfrogs and climb trees, his quick smile and playful nature. It was an infection caused by her father's whip that had taken him.

Papa Vandi, fully aware of Sadie's presence at the celebration, explained to her that Master Jacob had heard Tadeo reciting the alphabet and frantically tried to whip the knowledge from him. Sadie had not tutored Tadeo but had worked with his younger sister, Louisa, many times. *Had she indirectly led him to his death?* Overwhelmed, she fell to a heap in the corner while tears raced down her cheeks. Ellie came late that night to guide her back to the big house.

Sadie's parents' plans for the ball were in full force, and a happy frenzy around the preparations consumed the house. After Tadeo's funeral, Sadie avoided the shacks and the slaves. She snuck a few times to lay fresh flowers on his grave, never able to shake the idea that he was four years younger than her, and dead because of her. She wanted to somehow rescue her friends from their master, her father, teach them and feed them, and help them to fly freely just to see how far they could go. But then an image of Tadeo fading away inside a bag under the dirt reminded her of what happened when they tried. And so she evaded the big house and eluded the slave shacks and hid herself amongst the trees, finding refuge in being alone. This continued for days, but nobody bothered to look for her.

On an overcast and lazy Sunday afternoon, Isaiah approached Sadie as she sat drawing a large lunar moth on the leaf of a tree. He did not say anything, just reached for her hand. He pressed her fingers gently to his lips, barely touching them before intertwining them with his own. She turned to him and looked into his warm, thoughtful brown eyes. There she saw how they had missed each other.

She raised her lips to meet his. Their first kiss was soft and gentle. Eventually it led to more furtive kisses, urgent and hungry. From that moment on, they would steal away all the time they could find together. They kissed under moonbeams and held tightly to each other in dark corners and hidden sites, breathing each other in, discovering each other and themselves. Sadie brought him food, clothes, water, and anything else she could to keep him healthy and well. Freshly brewed sweet tea and warm bread with homemade jam were his favorites. Working with passion and zeal every day, Isaiah tried to keep Papa Vandi off his back and get to Sadie quickly each evening.

He worked on finalizing the plans with Sadie. They felt a new intensity and necessity to run away together. All they wanted was a patch of land to work, a small house for shelter, and a chance that was not normally in the stars for a slave boy and a master's daughter. Isaiah was cautious with every glance he made towards Sadie.

Sadie continued to smile and teach Mama Fato and the children, trying hard not to give away clues of her feelings or intentions. Sadie and Isaiah met in thick trees and faraway edges of the plantation, always scanning the surroundings and listening for approaching footsteps. In their eyes, they were soul mates, partners, and equals. Yet they realized that if anyone were to know of their relationship, they would be ruined.

A few weeks passed. Sadie ached to hear the story Mama Fato was whispering to her children as they drifted off to sleep on the scraps of blankets scattered around the dirt floor of the one-room cabin. Sadie crept into the cabin and reclaimed her place on the floor with eager ears. It was a story of a snail and a crab that were friends. One day, they were walking and playing on the beach when a sea gull flew overhead. There was a hole nearby, and the crab scrambled for it, leaving the snail out in the open as an easy prey for the sea gull. The sea gull swooped down and carried the snail away. The crab felt relieved that the sea gull was gone, but guilty that the snail had been eaten. He slowly made his way to the snail's home to share the bad news with the snail's mother. To his surprise, his friend the snail, was there to greet him at the door. The sea gull had told the snail to find a new friend and to never trust someone that put his own safety and well-being a priority above loyalty and decency. Holding on to each other is what is most important, no matter what evil lurks.

Sadie walked home that night in the darkness. The words echoed in her head, haunting her as if it were a boo hag tale rather than a simple bedtime story. She had crept into that house hundreds of times while the little ones drifted off to sleep to the soothing stories of Mama Fato. Normally, Mama Fato acted as if Sadie were one of her own. But on that evening, Mama Fato seemed to be looking at, and talking directly to, Sadie. The story became an accusation or a warning aimed right for Sadie's heart. And Sadie's heart, well that was something she worked very hard to keep hidden and protected. Even from Mama Fato.

Isaiah did not hear the incriminating story that evening, nonetheless Sadie knew he had heard it before. He worked in the fields with Papa Vandi, trying to finish the day's work before the sun set completely. His body aching and sweat dripping, he would sleep soundly as soon as he found his scrap on which to lay his head on the dirt floor.

Sadie thought about the small portion of bread and roots he probably ate for dinner compared to her own shrimp and buttered biscuits. She considered the hours she sat with her feet in the stream today as Ellie beat clothes on the rock besides her singing a sad song. Her mother's constant complaints about the loneliness and hardships of the plantation as she sat on the porch fanning herself all afternoon left a vile taste in Sadie's mouth. Sadie realized at once that she is the stupid crab from the story, deserving of every accusation Mama Fato had sent her way, and she certainly did not want to put any of them in the path of a sea gull. From the story, it was clear Mama Fato knew Sadie's and Isaiah's relationship had escalated.

Sadie wanted to run to her, to tell her everything, to attempt to describe the most extraordinary feelings she kept hidden inside, and her deepest desires for the future, but there was no need. Mama Fato already knew.

◆ ◆ ◆

The debutant ball took place on an enchanting evening in late September. Breathtaking in a white gown with soft pink trim, Sadie strolled out to the veranda as the guests arrived. She looked radiant with rosy cheeks, a quick, sincere smile, and proud, shimmering blue eyes. Her delicately curled hair hung long down her back in a neat and ornate barrette. She curtsied and made small talk, laughed, and complimented. She danced and perused the crowd.

None of the guests seemed to notice how often she looked out the windows towards the trees. Nobody noticed Isaiah in those very same trees watching her, smiling, admiring her beauty, and trying to contain his fear, excitement, and adrenaline for what was to come. The delightful melodies from the orchestra blew through the entire plantation that evening on a soft, southern breeze. Life would never be the same.

The party continued late into the night as stars shone brightly above. Then, the pace slowed, the music lowered, and guests began to wander to their carriages, content and ready for the journey home. Without warning, as she stood waving to departing guests, Sadie became violently ill. One horrific moment passed as she collapsed on the veranda and Isaiah watched helplessly from the trees.

They both realized that their plan to run away together in the chaotic aftermath and cleanup of the ball could not be put into action. They had hoped that the focus of the servants would be on returning the plantation to its normal state. Hoped that her parents would be distracted with endless discussions about the guests and potential suitors. But all the attention turned to Sadie.

Servants carried her to her room and changed her into a nightgown. Ellie wiped her down with cool water and pulled her hair back into a neat braid. Not only did Sadie feel too weak to get to Isaiah, all eyes were on her now. She was sick for days, vomiting, dizzy, and exhausted.

Sadie's parents feared she had caught something from the ball or from the swamplands where she spent way too much time. When Sadie showed no signs of improvement, Jacob sent for the doctor. Ellie said that Sadie was just worn down from the excitement and needed rest. Ellie sat with Sadie, bathed her, and fed her simple broth and biscuits to calm her stomach. She braided her hair and held her hand.

By moonlight, Ellie would sneak to the slave cabins and update Mama Fato on the happenings of the house. These smart women knew exactly what ailed young Sadie, and also knew it was only a matter of time before her own people came to know as well. They began devising a plan.

An outbreak of yellow fever, bad fortune for others in the south, worked in their favor by keeping the doctor away for a long time. Ellie approached Master Jacob with a request. She was concerned about the master and mistress and suggested she stay with Sadie in a quarantined wing of the house until the doctor could examine her. A hypochondriac, Jacob gave permission.

Over the course of forty-eight hours, Papa Vandi, Mama Fato, Ellie, and Isaiah worked together to plan an escape—a route to a hidden pathway with many helpful hands that could lead them to the North and the freedom they dreamed of so desperately. Isaiah revealed that Sadie had been describing it to him for years and had been giving him very specific details and directions for their recent hopes of escaping together. Mama Fato, Papa Vandi, and Ellie smiled and nodded. Then Papa Vandi offered suggestions of routes he had heard other slaves whisper about.

Mama Fato and the children would start out when the Thompson's were eating their evening meal, leaving their post in the fields watched over by Papa Vandi. He and Isaiah would meet up with them late at night, with Sadie. A risky plan, but it might work if executed well.

Stormy and incredibly hot, the afternoon leading into the escape arrived. Rain came in downpours. Sadie later laughed while telling Mama Fato that she came onto this plantation in a raging storm and left it behind in another.

In the early evening, Ellie secretly helped Sadie to the slave homes and kissed her goodbye. Sadie waited in the vacant cabin with a small bag packed with money, clothes, and food. She sat unmoving, thinking about all the stories and all the love that had happened within those meager walls.

When Papa Vandi and Isaiah arrived, she was ready to lead the way. Although there were no stars to follow that night, they were able to find the abandoned fishing shack where the rest of the family was waiting. Sadie and Isaiah lay huddled in a corner, clutching each other and listening to the rain wash their scent and their footprints away. They whispered prayers for strength, for this chance, for a new life. Isaiah stroked her cheek and told her over and over how much he loved her while Sadie curled into his chest and promised him they would make it—that this is what they were born to do. She yearned to live for him and be with him forever in a far away place. Each precious minute they spent nestled together, murmuring and dozing, empowered by faith and fear. In an attempt to get more miles between them and the plantation before morning, they left a few hours later heading northwest.

The group walked in alert silence. The children pushed themselves to walk at a quick pace, following the determined strides of Sadie and Mama Fato. The men followed at a distance, listening, watching, and waiting for any sign of trouble coming from what they had left behind. They walked for hours, taking short rests only when the children needed it. They stopped for sleep in the deep darkness of night, finding refuge in the thick trees. They drank fresh water from rivers and streams they stumbled across, and ate wild berries, nuts, and the meager supply of food they were able to pack. There were a few farmers and plantation workers who would leave food where they knew runaways might find it. And so it was that they would find a small pile of potatoes or stale cornbread.

Sadie knew freedom was a luxury. It touched her that there were others risking their own safety by trying to help Isaiah and his family find freedom. It inspired Sadie to know slaves had come this way before them and survived. Every quiet, aching step was one more step away from her purgatory, one more step away from the slaves' hell, and one more step closer to liberty. Each of them could feel it. Each of them tried to stay under control, but at times they wanted to just stop and breathe and dance and cheer and embrace one another without worry of a whipping.

Isaiah's sisters, Seba and Juba, made up a little song they mouthed over and over until the entire group was whispering along. "We are finding freedom and leaving the fields behind. No more whips, no more pain, only love and sunshine!"

Freedom beckoned. They could taste it. Their hearts pounded with persistent adrenaline, their hands shook in exultant anticipation. The group marched forward as a strong, steadfast army of believers. Steps blurred into miles, minutes turned to days. They were never sure where they were or how far they had traveled, but they were absolute in their destination. A Promised Land where they could work and live the lives they had been dreaming about for years. Together.

One night as the group rested, Sadie pulled Isaiah away and led him to a weeping willow very similar to the one she had sat beneath next to him what seemed like a lifetime ago. She breathed deeply and closed her eyes.

"What is it?" he whispered.

"Izzy, our baby deserves this. We have to make it. He can never know that life. He can never see you like that."

Isaiah placed a hand over Sadie's stomach and rubbed softly. For a long while they just sat together under the tree, so much to say and so much felt, but no words coming to them. Finally, as the group stirred nearby, Isaiah said, "I promise. You, him, me, we will do this. He will never know anything but good."

He kissed her stomach and then her lips before rising to his feet, helping her to hers, and holding the drooping branches out of her way. They headed back to the group and on with their journey.

They walked hand in hand for some time before he let her go to the front of the assembly, and he fell behind next to Papa.

Papa nudged him with an elbow, "You know you got to marry that girl."

"Oh, I will do that, Papa."

"I can't help but notice the 'he's' coming out of you mouths."

"Sadie is positive it is a boy, and I just listen to her," Isaiah responded proudly.

Papa smiled. "I understand."

Eight days into the escape and about ninety miles away from the plantation, trouble arrived. A constable of the law hired and paid for by Jacob raced through the woods on horseback with two other monsters of men. The birds above gave a piercing warning, and the group ran in all directions. For one long second, Sadie and Isaiah made eye contact. Between them passed love, thanks, permission, and promise. Then back to the plan. She blew him a kiss and turned to run. He touched his hand to his heart and turned to fight.

Sadie covered her stomach with folded arms and raced into the trees. The children had been told to run and hide until Mama Fato called for them. Crouched in hollow logs, perched in branches, and buried in twigs and leaves, they stayed safe and silent. Mama Fato became part of the thicket, and Sadie blended with the creek bank in a shallow ravine. Papa Vandi and Isaiah stood ready to defend them.

"There you are, Papa. I've been looking for you!" screamed a raspy voice. A whip made contact with flesh. A strained cry and chains clanked. Then the heart-wrenching scream of a little girl devastated the air. From their hiding places, the family recognized the voice of seven-year-old Kizzy, whom Sadie had seen climbing a tree just moments before.

"I know there are more of ya niggers out here," the raspy voice called out with glee, "and I will be sending more of my men for each and every one of ya. They are already on the way. But I'm gonna take these boys back where they belong, and for this stupid child, well she'll show ya what will become of all ya when I catch back up."

A gunshot rang out. Then they heard the dreadful thud of the little girl's body collapsing lifeless on the dirt.

"No!" bawled Papa Vandi's booming voice before the foot of the constable crashed into the devastated man's jaw. The male slaves were pushed onto the back of a horse, and their restrained cries and labored breathing could be heard by all their hidden loved ones. Then the horses took off, the chains confining Isaiah and Papa Vandi rattling with every bounce, until the gallops faded away into complete and utter silence.

After twenty terrifying minutes passed in hiding, Mama Fato began to sing. Cautiously, the children and Sadie came together. They made a simple grave, whispered a heartfelt prayer for Kizzy, and traveled on. Tears fell. Bodies ached. Despair reigned. Yet they walked and hid. Walked and hid, accepting what was offered in terms of shelter and food, thanking only with nods and hand squeezes. They trudged along in a dreamlike trance. Safe houses came and went, and time was relentless. Sadie's delicate condition became more prominent.

The constable had made it clear he would hunt them down and bring them all back to justice. That fear kept them moving forward. They were acutely aware of every twig snap and bird call. They took turns standing sentry while the children slept. They never stopped watching and waiting for the moment whips and chains would catch up to them.

The group of refugees had no idea how long it had taken Jacob to realize Sadie was missing and not quarantined. Ellie had sworn to wait as long as possible to report her as vanished. Did the value and strength of Papa Vandi and Isaiah in the fields protect them from being punished too brutally for running? Wouldn't Sadie having gone missing put them in even more of a vulnerable and hopeless position? What had become of the men? Would they try to run again? Was that even possible now that Jacob had to be on high alert? Questions haunted the minds of both Mama Fato and Sadie, although they rarely discussed them. Their time was spent caring for the children, giving love and encouragement and hope, and pushing them forward.

It had taken the constable eight days to track down and capture Isaiah and Papa Vandi. It took five months for Sadie, Mama Fato, and the children to reach the city of Detroit, the final stop on the Underground Railroad in the United States. There, they soon found a small, safe, and cozy home on the third floor of a wealthy and kind family. Sadie worked as their governess and Mama Fato as their cook. They huddled together, cared for each other, and prayed every night for the men to somehow find them. They were alive and free, but, without their loves, they were merely surviving.

They consoled each other, Mama Fato repeating that this choice was right, they deserved this new life, and this is what Papa Vandi and Isaiah would want for them. The children were growing and flourishing in the new environment filled with calm and opportunity, while the women worked, provided, and kept their desolation hidden.

◆ ◆ ◆

Late at night, Mama Fato could hear Sadie weeping, whispering to Isaiah for forgiveness, and praying. "Please protect him, Father, and give him the chance to know our baby. Bless Papa and Izzy with hope and help them to stand brave and resilient together. Let them feel your endless love and the love from all of us and never give up. Thank you for Mama Fato and this family. Please protect and watch over each of us. Somehow, someday, please bring us all together. In Your name, Amen."

Sadie gave birth to a son, John Isaiah Vandi, on March 5, 1851. It was an easy labor and delivery, and Mama Fato stood by her side through it all. Healthy and strong with a full head of soft hair, an angelic face, and deep, observant eyes, John Isaiah was beautiful. He knew nothing but love. All of his little aunts and uncles adored him, his grandmother told stories to him every night, and his mother sang sweet melodies that soothed him into peaceful dreams. He would face prejudice but never experience the horrors under which he was conceived. He was his parents' impossible dream come true. He was free.

The family settled into a routine of work and study together, and there were moments when they almost felt complete. They lived a simple, valuable life. They had everything they needed to stay warm and nourished. For the children, memories of the plantation began to fade. Fewer and fewer conversations were about the past. Even Mama Fato and Sadie began to relax about being recognized and discovered in town. They became more established among the servants in the city and more able to trust and look strangers in the eyes. Over time, they could acknowledge the wonder of the stars or the beauty of the trees and lose themselves in the moment without feeling the need to know where they could run and hide if the constable appeared. The children laughed freely. The family had picnics and went for walks and read real books each night by candlelight. They were more than surviving; they were thriving. They were growing up free.

Baby John was fifteen months old when Sadie kissed him goodbye. She left silently by moonlight while the family slept, leaving behind her beloved child, a small pile of coins, and a letter addressed to Mama Fato. At sunrise Mama Fato arose, checked on all the slumbering children, and discovered the letter. In many ways, she had been expecting it. She sat down to read at the kitchen table with shaking hands. Mama Fato had the ability to read because of Sadie's patience and her own determination. She, and most of her children, had struggled to freedom, and Sadie had been their loyal ally. Yet, she already had a feeling the letter could be the last she knew of that caring girl.

My Dearest Mama Fato,

I want you to know I am so proud to be loved by you and honored that you have allowed me to be part of your family. You are the bravest and most extraordinary woman I have ever known. I have watched you and admired you for as long as I can remember and have learned that family is not blood, it is love. As a Thompson, I knew nothing of love, as a Vandi, it is all I have ever felt and all I was ever given. I am eternally grateful.

I know you will understand I must go back. I cannot and will not be the crab. No matter what happens to me. I have to try to hold Isaiah again and tell him of our son. We will do everything we can to get to you and to John and will not leave Papa Vandi behind. Thank you for watching over John for me. He is in the most glorious of hands with you and will learn all he needs from you. If I am not able to bring Isaiah and Papa back to you, I know John will bring you joy, and through him, you will always have us and our love.

Most Truly Yours,
Sadie

Back on the plantation, the outbreak of yellow fever had kept the doctor away for longer than expected. The Thompson's safely worried on the other side of their estate. Ellie kept her end of the bargain. She cleaned laundry, prepared sweet tea each afternoon and meals throughout the day. She ran baths and sang calming spirituals for days to a pillow so the Thompson's would never suspect Sadie's disappearance.

Eleven days after Sadie's escape, three days after Isaiah and Papa Vandi had returned in the middle of yet another stormy night, Ellie frantically ran to her master and mistress screaming that dear Miss Sadie was gone. She explained that she had gone to check on her by candlelight as she had done every few hours, only to find a vacant bed. Ellie's whole body was shaking and tears flowed down her cheeks. Jacob stirred up a search party to comb the nearby woods with no inclination that his daughter was over a hundred miles away and across state lines, let alone that she carried the child of a slave in her womb.

The next morning, a fatal mistake occurred. Ellie had finished taking the clean sheets off the line and was stopping to pick fresh flowers for Miss Sadie's anticipated return on her way back up to the house when Isaiah approached. He walked with a limp and his face looked well beaten, but there was no denying his smile. Ellie nodded his way and stooped to pick one more yellow wildflower.

"What are you smiling at, boy? What do you have to be happy about? Did you have something to do with this? You tell me now or die!" roared Jacob from the veranda.

"I not know what you talking about, sir. Just smiling at a lady picking pretty flowers on a pretty day is all," Isaiah replied.

"I can see it in your eyes. Tell me where she is! Tell me now!" Jacob ran down, grabbed Isaiah, and began punching and kicking him while continuing to scream.

Isaiah tried to hold back his rage, but it overcame him. Heedless of the danger, he lost control, threw Master Thompson hard against a tree, and while pinning him against it, said, "Since when do you care where she is? She gone and never comin' back."

"String this boy up, y'all!" Jacob shrieked. Anger pulsed throughout his body.

Within moments, Isaiah's arms were twisted and tied behind his back, and a noose was being tightened around his neck. Two men swung the other end of the rope around a thick branch of the very same tree against which he had pinned his master. With a furious nod from Jacob, the men pulled hard on the rope lifting Isaiah into the air. Isaiah fought for his life. He gasped and kicked, wriggled and reached, to no avail. Life slowly left his aching body as he stared at the clouds above.

Isaiah swung there on the middle of the plantation as workers went on with their duties and the sun meandered across the sky. Ellie watched the whole episode. She was the one who lowered him down. She was the one who beat the drum to alert others of a death and a burial. She was the one who squeezed Papa Fato in a tight embrace knowing that the last of his loved ones on this plantation was now gone forever, the second of his children he had seen dead in a week. Ellie was also the one to lay the fresh flowers she had originally picked for Sadie's empty room on the fresh grave.

In her heart and whispered prayers, Ellie questioned the meaning and purpose of his life. He had been born to sweat and bleed and toil for a man only to be killed by him. As Isaiah's friend, she knew there had been so much potential and passion and hope within him. Ellie left flowers on his grave every day. She left them, not just for her friend, but for his love, Sadie, the baby she carried, Mama Fato, Papa Vandi, and everyone else who lost a piece of themselves the day Isaiah died.

Papa Vandi was never the same. He worked feverishly and forced all the slaves around him to do the same. He led them with a brutal intensity. He did not look anyone in the eye, and kept to himself. He refused to visit the cemetery, and did not even blink when the drum beat to recognize another death. He went through the rituals of life. He ate, drank, labored, slept, and breathed, but he was a lost and empty man. Until he saw Miss Sadie come home.

Sadie had been gone almost two years. She arrived by carriage, wearing an elegant yellow dress and bonnet. She strode up the steps of her former home. The slave cabins, once her sanctuary, had been burned down by her father in a fit of rage.

When no slaves could recall seeing Sadie leave and not return, he had taken his revenge with fire. Sadie noticed it right away, but did not react to it. In her face, she showed no emotion.

Sadie let herself into the house without knocking, nodded politely at her mother crocheting in the sitting room, and found her father looking over papers in his study. Her mother began screaming, "Sadie, Sadie, you are home, dear!" and attempted to put her arms around her. Sadie gave her mother such a look of such disdain that she backed away and left the room, tears running down her perfectly rouged face.

"Good afternoon, Father. I am here for one purpose and one purpose only. I want to buy Papa Vandi and Isaiah. I am able to offer you twice what I know you paid for Papa, and the same amount for Isaiah. I want you to sign them over to me in a legal contract, and then let us go in peace."

"Who do you think you are, Sadie? You are a dishonor and disgrace to this family. How dare you leave and then come back with such a proposition? You need to take your place here. You need to gain some discipline and decency and pray that society, as well as your own mother and I, will accept you back." Jacob's voice shook and his face was a brilliant red.

"I have no interest in your views of decency and no desire to ever be part of your society. I just want those men. Do we have a deal?" Sadie's voice was calm.

A long moment of silence passed. Jacob looked her over in disgust. Standing in the same room, they both realized how very far apart they were from each other. There was nothing to cling to, nothing to understand.

"Well, Isaiah is just rotting bones in the nigger cemetery by now. You give me what you offered for both men for Papa Vandi, get the hell off my property, and we have a deal."

Jacob gathered papers from a drawer, sat back down at his desk, and began organizing the documents of the transaction while Sadie sat tall in her chair. She waited as he signed off on his prized slave. Finally, he rose and handed her the binding agreement. Choking down her emotion, Sadie folded the papers into her purse, set the money in a neat pile on the desk, and walked out of her father's study without looking back.

When she stepped on the porch, she no longer had to act the role and began to run towards the fields, searching for the man who was both her family and her property, wanting to get him off this land and away from this perdition.

"Papa...Papa!" Sadie cried as loudly as she could. Moments later, Papa Vandi heard her.

"Sadie, Sadie, is that you?" They saw each other across a rice field. She raced towards him.

Ellie later described this reunion as a beautiful moment. A long hug along with ever-flowing tears and all kinds of explanations and information shared. Papa Vandi swept Sadie into the air with pure joy and love on his face. This was the reaction of a father whose daughter has returned; the reaction of a slave just offered freedom; the reaction of a husband on a quest to return to his beloved wife.

But Sadie also needed to say goodbye to Isaiah and leave the dream of walking off this plantation with him behind her. At his makeshift grave, Sadie knelt to leave a lock of baby John's curly brown hair. She kissed the grass and whispered something only Isaiah could hear, and then she stood and reached for Papa Vandi's hand. They walked away from the cemetery with fingers intertwined back towards the carriage they thought would take them to the North—take them home.

Ellie had been watching from afar. As they prepared to leave, she went back to polishing the silver in the dining room. She heard Master Jacob raid the liquor cabinet and gulp down his favorite whiskey. Then, she heard him open the front door. Through the window, Ellie saw him raise his Kentucky Flintlock pistol at the same moment Miss Sadie saw it. Before Papa Vandi could stop her, she let go of his hand and jumped in front of him.

Jacob wore a crazed smile as he cocked the pistol and fired. The bullet hit Sadie in the chest. Papa Vandi caught her as she collapsed and lowered her gently to the ground. He glared at Jacob and then brushed the hair out Sadie's beautiful face. The puddle of blood soaked into the dirt, and he knew she was gone.

Jacob pulled back the steel striking slab and the flint striker and put in another bullet. He aimed for Papa Vandi as the slave wept over Sadie. Ellie watched as Master Jacob clenched and gasped and fought the demons in his head, finally dropping the pistol to the ground and turning back into the house. Papa Vandi picked up Sadie and carried her into the woods. Moments later, the drums began.

Miss Sadie was buried in the slave cemetery, in a simple grave next to Isaiah, marked by rocks and shells arranged by the shaking hands of Papa Vandi. That night, a violent storm fulminated.

If Mistress Thompson realized what had happened, she never said. The only true witness, Ellie's discretion in the matter, helped to ensure her own future freedom. In his will, Jacob wrote that upon his death Ellie would be freed.

As a free woman, Ellie would tell stories to her own grandchildren about the lovely ghost that would enchant the plantation wearing a shimmering yellow dress. The ghost could often be seen sitting in the ruins of the slave shacks waiting for a story to be told under the stars, strolling along the water's edge, or dancing in the moonlight. "That girl," she would say, "was nothing but good and beautiful trapped in a bad and ugly world."

Papa Vandi continued to lead the slaves in their work, Sadie's signed contract always delicately folded and tucked into his pocket. The knowledge that the surviving members of his family thrived, liberated, under the care of Mama Fato, kept him strong. Isaiah and Sadie were together, their love hidden and protected under stones for all of time, and their child happy and free. Papa Vandi died a few weeks before the Proclamation was signed. Never has the funeral drum beat louder or singing rung more passionately amongst the slaves than in celebration of his life.

Mama Fato worked hard. She raised six children and the first of many grandchildren. She lived long, loved deeply, and sang sadly. She left her mark in the world with the stories she told and the scattering of children she could never hug enough. She knew they owed their freedom, in part, to Isaiah's and Sadie's sacrifices.

The Thompson plantation still stands today. Enchanting, its inglorious history contrasts with its ethereal beauty. It is privately owned, but some of the trees the slaves once walked under still stand. One can still hear the echoes of laughter and sense the anguish in the soil. Weather and time have damaged the slave cemetery. Grave markers are worn and ragged, and broken stones, shells, and splintered wood are scattered on the ground. It remains an eerie and troubling place, yet sacred and worthy of remembrance.

136 AUBURN LANE

Donna Hill

IT WAS THE WINTER OF 1932. The only sign of life on the empty streets was the wino wrapped in a filthy gray blanket that blended with the dull gray buildings and the proverbial gray sky that always seemed to hang over the hill. Martha realized he wasn't a ball of trash because he reached out, scared the shit out of her, and begged for a penny or a nickel. Martha didn't have either one. All she had was an address—136 Auburn Lane.

The row of tenements sat on a hill. When you got to the top and dropped down to the other side, you'd left Harlem and entered the Bronx. 136 Auburn sat right in the middle, almost like a way station. For the most part, it didn't matter one way or the other. Up the hill or down, everybody was broke, poor or worse.

Martha hugged her brown cardboard suitcase close to her chest. Not so much that she was worried about it being stolen but more to keep the wind from sliding under her buttonless coat and making its acquaintance with her thin cotton dress. She checked the addresses on the lifeless buildings against the slip of paper that the woman at The Center had written down—136 Auburn Lane.

She'd lived at The Center for nearly a year, right after she'd lost her job and then her apartment. She'd spent a week riding back and forth on the elevated number 4 train until the motorman found her curled up asleep, hungry and smelling, and told her she had to get off. But not before he told her about The Center and how they help people who are in a bad way. Place must be overrun, she'd thought at the time, cause everywhere she looked people were in a bad way.

You see, at the height of the Great Depression, nobody had nothing. Even white folks were broke. So broke, some of them jumped out of windows to end the agony of being poor. Colored folks, on the other hand, were used to making something out of nothing as a regular way of life. So this depression was simply an extra dose of already bad days.

Martha peered into the dimness trying to make out the faded numbers. Even the streetlights seemed depressed, barely offering a flicker. 136 Auburn Lane, the last tenement on the street, stood by itself, separated from 134 by an alley. Beyond 136—the Bronx. Martha wasn't going to the Bronx.

She stood in front of the narrow building and imagined the rooms must be extra tiny. She let her eyes count the dark floors. Six. The note from the center read: *1st floor Apt A1. Ask for Mr. Smart.* The rusted black gate that guarded the broken concrete path that led to the front door cried in protest when she pushed it open, then screeched shut with a click of its own volition.

Martha kept her eyes on the cracked concrete beneath her feet, not wanting the loose sole on her right shoe to get caught and made worse before she could find some gum or glue, if she was lucky, to hold it together.

The double entry door had been made of a combination of warped wood and wrought iron that had rusted to a deep orange. There were no bells. There was no knob. Martha pushed the door open. It, unlike the front gate, opened without a sound. The slim hallway had apartments on either side with just enough space to squeeze by your neighbor on the opposite side if they opened their door at the same time. Mr. Smart's apartment was the first one on the left.

Martha set her suitcase at her feet, straightened out her coat, and tried to smooth the wrinkles out of her dress. She knocked two times, and before she could lower her hand, the door swung inward. Her hand that hung in midair jumped to her chest.

"You must be Martha. I'm Leroy Smart." He grinned and a gold incisor winked at her. But that wasn't what struck her as odd. The odd thing was that Leroy Smart was decked out in a suit and tie, starched white shirt, and spit-shined black wing-tipped shoes. He stood out in stark contrast against the gray backdrop like his incisor stood out against the uncannily white teeth.

"Yes. Martha Hopewell."

"Liz at The Center told me all about you."

She wanted to ask if that meant he knew she had a drinking problem, which was the real reason she'd lost her job and then her apartment and wound up sleeping on the train and then wound up on a cot at The Center. But if she took her pills, she didn't need to drink, and the strange ideas stayed out of her head. She'd been dry for five whole months. Her sobriety coin was tucked in her bra. *So what if he knew?* Liz had said everything had been taken care of. She believed Liz.

Leroy partly closed the door to reach behind it for keys hung on a hook. He dangled the keys in front of her like a carrot in front of a horse. "I'll show you your room. I'm sure you want to get settled."

Their attention was diverted to the bump, thump, bump on the precarious staircase. A dark-coated man with a short-brimmed fedora tilted low over his face dragged a large suitcase down the stairs. Leroy's slits for eyes followed the progress. Neither man shared a word of acknowledgement. The front door closed silently behind him.

Leroy's incisor sparkled. He lifted his chin in the direction of the stairs. "After you. Top floor."

Martha inwardly groaned and hoped her bad right knee would act right for the trip. She gripped the thin wooden rail and pulled herself up the six flights of stairs. By flight four, a thin sheen of perspiration coated her forehead. Her lungs scolded her by flight five. By the time she reached her floor, her knee howled. Oddly enough, with two apartments to every floor, there wasn't a scent of dinner cooking or blues playing or the sounds of everyday life behind the doors. It was soundless and odorless as if nothing existed.

If Martha hadn't been so tired, if her right knee hadn't hurt so bad, if she hadn't felt so cold, and if she hadn't promised herself she would never go back to The Center, she would have told Mr. Smart 'no thanks' before he ever opened her door to 6A.

The scent of yesterday and the day before sat in dusty corners almost as if afraid to make its presence known. Apartment 6A was no more than a square room with a sink, stove and battered refrigerator no taller than a four-year old pressed against one wall. Missing doors on the shelves looked back at her with echoing emptiness. A twin bed rested forlornly against the other wall. The single bulb in the center of the room cast the space into a permanent state of dimness.

"Bathroom is right behind that door," Mr. Smart said with an enthusiasm of one who'd found money in an old purse.

Martha pretended to smile and did not dare imagine what might be behind door number one. Instead she walked to the sink and turned on the water. The pipes clanged and chugged violently before they spewed out a tan stream of water. Martha's stomach roiled.

"Oh don't you worry about that. Clears right up after you run the water for a while."

Martha gave him a halfhearted smile.

In the distance a thump, thump, thump could be heard. The same sound as when that nameless man dragged the suitcase down the stairs. Maybe he was moving, Martha surmised. *What other reason could anyone have for dragging suitcases down the stairs this time of the night?*

"Thank you, Mr. Smart."

"Anything you need you let me know. You can start work tomorrow morning. I wouldn't expect you to start tonight." His incisor winked, and then he was gone leaving Martha alone with the grayness and the silence.

Silence except for the intermittent thump, thump, thump.

The sun didn't seem to shine above 136 Auburn Lane. Rather it looked at the building from the side, its rays at a slant found its way right into Martha's sixth floor apartment.

She blinked against the glare and slowly pushed herself up from the two-inch-thick mattress. She didn't trust the dingy sheets that were on the bed, so she'd slept on top of one of her dresses and covered herself with her coat. Martha tested out her knee. It gave a bit of protest sounding like a knuckle being cracked when she stood, but overall it felt pretty good. She briskly rubbed her hands up and down her arms and went to peek out the window. Nothing to see but more tenements headed toward the Bronx. Martha turned in a slow circle and took in her space. *Yes. It looked just as dismal in the daylight.*

Three sudden sharp knocks on her door accelerated her heart. Her bare feet slap slapped against the wood floor. "Yeah?" she inquired from the safety of her side of the locked door.

"Mornin'."

It was Mr. Smart. She cracked the door open. Only one eye and the side of her nose and mouth were exposed.

"We need to go over your duties."

She'd barely rubbed the sleep out of her eyes. "Um...can you give me a... minute?"

"Only a moment. You need to get started."

From the slit in the door, she saw him check his watch and then the space over his shoulder. What was more curious was that he was fully dressed in a business suit, shirt, and tie, and those wing-tipped shoes. *Who dressed like that this time of the morning?* Martha shut the door. She shuffled to the bathroom and turned on the faucets.

The pipes banged in protest refusing to give up the water until a brown gush broke free, slowly turned yellow then cleared. Gurgled. Martha stuck her finger under the water. Lukewarm. She splashed water on her face, rinsed her mouth, and dried her hands and face on a dingy towel that hung on a nail. She peered into the dull mirror and ran her hand across her head then down her wrinkled dress. This was the best she could do for the moment. She returned to the bed and slid her feet into her shoes.

Three sharp knocks on the door.

"I'm coming. I'm coming." She pulled the door open.

Mr. Smart's nondescript face had contorted into rows of wrinkles and frowns of annoyance as if he'd been waiting for the better part of the morning instead of five minutes. He smiled, making his face a disconcerting combination of rage and benevolence. Martha felt queasy.

"Right this way. We will start on the first floor and work our way up."

Martha mentally groaned. Much like the night before, the building was devoid of smell other than the scent of something old and discarded. *Where were the scents and sounds of people getting ready for the day? Bacon frying, coffee brewing, voices shouting? Nothing. Not a gotdamn peep. Quiet as a tomb, as her grandmother used to say.*

"You'll start on the ground floor, then go up to the top and work your way down. In. That. Order." He opened a narrow door she hadn't noticed before. It was packed with mops and brooms, sponges, buckets and black garbage bags, cleaning solutions and huge, industrial sized bottles of disinfectant. "Everything you need. The entryway must be swept, mopped, and disinfected twice per day, the hallways and the stairs, too, from top to bottom. If any garbage is set outside any of the apartment doors, you gather it up and dump it in the incinerator. Don't open them for any reason."

Martha blinked in confusion. *Why would she open anybody's trash?* "Are there tenants in any of the apartments?" She had yet to see a soul or hear a sound, except for the man and his suitcase last night.

His incisor flashed. "Of course."

Martha tried to calculate how many times she would have to go up and down the stairs. Her head started to pound.

"Now, you need to be finished with the morning cleaning by 8 a.m. and the evening by 6 p.m. During the day there may be some... deliveries. But don't concern yourself. I'll take care of it. The trash cans need to be set out on the curb Monday, Wednesday and Friday nights by eight for pickup." He stepped closer and lowered his voice. "There is a special pickup on Tuesday and Thursday, but don't concern yourself with that. I'll take care of it." He paused and the corners of his eyes tightened. "It is very important that you get the days and the times correct. Do you understand?"

His delivered his instructions in an even, almost pleasant, tone. That wasn't what was giving Martha the shakes. It was the look in his eyes. Something ugly. In that moment, she fully believed that if she didn't follow his orders to the letter, he would find a way to make her regret it. Then there was that smile again as if all was well with the world.

"I'll let you get started. You're already behind schedule." He reached into the pocket of his suit jacket and pulled out a slip of paper. He handed it to Martha. "In case you forget." With that, he walked away and entered his apartment.

Martha listened to the locks click into place and then nothing. Dead silence. She opened the folded piece of paper. On it was the typed schedule he'd told her about. Martha licked her dry lips, and a desperate urge for a drink hit her as if she'd been pushed. She gripped the banister and pulled in a long, deep breath. For a moment, she shut her eyes and visualized her sobriety coin. She could do this. Her only other option was to return to The Center, and that would mean she had failed, couldn't cut it. This place, as unsettling as it was, presented a chance for her to turn her life around. There were plenty of people out there that only wished they had this chance. That's what Liz at The Center kept telling her.

Martha glanced up at the winding staircase. If she started now, with any luck, she would be finished before the day was over. She gathered the supplies from the narrow closet and poured a cleaning solution from an unmarked white bottle into the bucket, then filled it with water from the slop sink. Loaded down with a broom, mop and bucket, she slowly made her way to the top floor.

What she needed was a plan. She'd start at the back of the hallway and work her way forward then down. The problem was she only had one bucket of water. Consequently, after the top floor, she would have to wash all the rest in the same dirty water. There was no way she planned to empty and refill the bucket after each floor. Mr. Smart couldn't possibly want her to do that. For a moment she stood still, catching her breath while contemplating her dilemma.

That's when she noticed, tucked along the side of the hallway, a door that didn't look like an apartment door. Maybe it was another utility closet with a sink.

She listened for any sound. She heard no more than her own breathing and scrambled thoughts. This did not surprise her. She tiptoed over to the closet, half expecting a door to open and someone to ask what the hell she was doing.

Nothing. Silence.

Martha reached for the knob, and the hairs on the back of her neck tingled. She hesitated. She thought she heard a noise like something being dragged. Something heavy.

A door on the fifth floor opened and shut. She inched over to the stairs and tried to look down without being noticed. It was the man from the night before. Her pulse began to race. She ducked back to avoid being seen and knocked over the bucket of water. The scent of Pine Sol filled the air and spread across the worn wood floor and under her feet. She felt the warm water ooze between the loose sole of her shoe.

Thump. Thump. Thump.

She pressed her back against the wall, wanting to disappear, as an inexplicable sensation of dread spread through her as surely as the water that pooled along the hallway. How long she stood there with her body as rigid as a corpse, she wasn't sure. But the next thing she heard was silence.

Martha's foot squished inside her shoe as she went about mopping up the mess she'd made. If she'd had any intention of making this one trip up and one trip down, she'd been mistaken.

After she'd gotten up the water as best she could, she started on the stairs with the wet mop. It amazed her how filthy the mop became when it seemed no one ever came up or down—other than the man with the suitcases. She wondered how much longer it would take him to move out, and why her hands were shaking.

By the time she'd reached the fourth floor, the mop was unusable unless she rinsed it and refilled her bucket. She trudged down to the ground floor and started the process over again. When she was finally done more than two hours later, every muscle in her body ached and she had yet to see, or hear, a single soul.

Martha returned to her one-room apartment and all but collapsed atop the single mattress. She felt exhausted. Her stomach knotted in hunger, and she was certain that the toddler refrigerator didn't hold anything of worth beyond the echo of empty.

With great effort, she pulled herself into an upright position. She had a few hours of free time before she had to start the cleaning all over again. She changed her wet socks and added some newspaper into the shoe with the loose sole, grabbed her coat and purse, and went in search of something to eat. If she remembered correctly, there was a small corner store about two blocks away.

With winter, twilight comes early. For some reason, it seemed to come even earlier to Auburn Lane. As early as three in the afternoon, an uncomfortable dimness dulled the walls, the stairs, and the bulbs that hung from the ceiling hardly gave up any light. Martha pulled her coat tightly around her and tiptoed down the stairs. With every step she took her heart raced faster and faster. An uncanny dread permeated her limbs as if the mere thought of creating a sound would render her...she wasn't sure.

She reached the front door and froze. He was coming down again.

Thump. Thump. Thump.

Martha's instinct to run kicked in, but she couldn't seem to get her feet to follow her brain.

The man appeared on the landing. His hat was still pulled low over his face obscuring his features. Martha pressed herself against the wall, wishing she could disappear.

He dragged the suitcase across her freshly washed floors. He never made eye contact and walked right passed her and out the front door. A cold breeze brushed her.

Martha swallowed over the dry knot in her throat. She stood in the doorway and watched the man with the suitcase. He walked down the pathway to the front gate and left without looking back.

Her heart hammered in her chest. It was hard to breathe. *Who was he, and what was in those suitcases?* She reached for the knob just as a door behind her opened.

"Going out?"

Martha turned. Mr. Smart, dressed in his formal wear, stood in his doorway.

"I was, uh, going to get something to eat."

He flashed a smile that didn't reach his eyes. "I see." He took a quick look around. "Finished cleaning?"

"Yes. For the morning."

"Hmm. Don't be gone too long. Time can get away from you." He stepped back inside and shut the door.

Martha shook off the chill that ran along her spine and stepped outside. She walked along Auburn Lane toward the corner, away from the Bronx. The store, if she remembered correctly, was about a block away. The street, even in the daytime, looked desolate. The impact of the Great Depression could be seen in the shabbiness of everything around her. What troubled Martha the most was the lack of people. It was as if some entity had scooped every one up and taken them away. *Ridiculous. On a cold day, anyone with good sense was indoors.* That explanation made sense. Not the foolishness in her head that made her believe something was very wrong on Auburn Lane.

The corner store, nothing more than a hole in the wall, did not impress her. Dust coated the practically bare shelves. The fruit, if you could still call it fruit, was withered and bruised. She could not find anyone in the store. *Where had the clerk gone?*

"What can I do for you?"

Martha yelped and grabbed her chest.

A middle-aged man appeared from behind a row of shelves.

"I...I was hoping to buy something to eat." Her gaze jumped around the store.

"Not much here as you can see." He ambled over to the counter, reached below and pulled out a bottle of bourbon.

Martha's eyes lit up.

The shopkeeper took a dull glass from under the counter and poured himself a drink. "Join me?"

Her mouth watered. She shoved her hands into the pockets of her coat to keep herself from snatching the glass out of his hand and downing the contents. Five months felt like a lifetime. She balled her hands into fists, took one step toward the counter, and then another. The shopkeeper smiled and produced another glass. Poured. Slid the glass toward Martha.

Her fingers uncurled in her pockets and shook as they reached for the glass. Every warning bell rang in her head. She licked her lips.

"Go on. Take a sip. Been a while since I had someone to drink with."

Her long fingers wrapped around the glass. The contents sloshed as she slowly brought it toward her mouth. The scent was intoxicating. Her lids fluttered over her eyes as she brought the glass to her lips.

The first sip burned and hummed all the way down. The jolt of it was a shock to her system. Her stomach almost rebelled but didn't, remembering its old friend. She sighed as the warmth spread through her limbs. When she opened her eyes, he was staring at her.

"Joe," he said, by way of introduction.

"Martha," she managed.

He raised his glass to her and finished off the contents.

Martha did the same. The powerful liquor went straight to her head, and all the events of the past two days became fuzzy and silly.

Joe refilled her glass.

She shouldn't. The warning bells rang loud. But they weren't loud enough to drown out the need that had sat like an unfed beast in her belly.

Joe walked away and disappeared into a back room. He returned moments later with a brown paper bag. He pushed it toward Martha.

Through the fuzz in her head she saw it was filled with packs of lunch meat, bread, eggs, apples, and a slab of bacon. Her mouth opened and closed. Her gaze landed on Joe's face that seemed to shift from his, to Mr. Smart, to the man with the suitcase, and then back again. *Ridiculous. It was the bourbon.*

"Ain't often I get company."

Martha blinked. "I don't have enough for all that," she stuttered, envisioning the five dollars in her pocket.

"Consider it payment for your company."

Martha stared at the bag. Her stomach rumbled.

"Take it." It sounded like more of a command than an offer.

Martha snatched up the bag and held it tight to her chest. "Thank you."

He grinned. That's when she noticed his gold incisor. Her head started to pound.

"Stop by anytime, Martha."

Martha backed away. Joe kept staring and smiling. She spun and practically ran out the door.

The cold wind slapped her in the face and momentarily cleared her head. Wildly she looked around. She was the only one on the street. The only one. Not even a stray cat. She double-timed it back to 136, pushed through the gate, and hurried up the lane, intermittently glancing over her shoulder, not sure what she was expecting to see, but she looked anyway.

The front door silently opened. Mr. Smart was standing in the entryway.

Her pulse raced. Guilt mixed with sweat began to cover her body.

"I see you met Joe."

Her mouth twitched as she tried to form words over the irrational fear that gripped her insides.

Martha hugged her bag close, lowered her head, and moved passed him toward the stairs.

"Don't let the evening cleanup get away from you," he said to her back.

"I won't," she mumbled and hurried up the stairs as fast as her bad knee would take her.

By the time she reached her apartment, she was shaking all over. She locked the door and slid the chain in place. For several moments she stood staring at the door, expecting at any moment for Mr. Smart to coming knocking, or worse.

Tears filled her eyes. *What was this place, this neighborhood where no one seemed to exist? Where was everyone? Where were all the people Liz said she'd sent here?*

That's what she needed to do. She needed to find a phone and call Liz and tell her to get her the hell out of here. But that would mean going back outside into the nothingness of this godforsaken neighborhood to find a pay phone that worked. The fright and the liquor had her head spinning. She needed food and time to think.

Martha took the brown paper bag and brought it over to the narrow kitchen counter. She emptied the contents. If she planned right, the food would last her a few days, at least until she got in touch with Liz.

She dared to open the tiny refrigerator and, to her surprise, found it pristine inside. She put the eggs and bacon on the one shelf, fixed herself a bologna sandwich, and wished she had something to wash it down with. The taste of the bourbon still lingered on the back of her tongue. *Come back anytime.*

She lifted a small plastic bottle from the bottom of the bag. It was filled with liquid. She unscrewed the cap. The scent of bourbon wafted to her nose. Her lids slid down over her eyes in a moment of euphoria. When she opened her eyes, she found herself staring down into the small circular opening at the tempting deep golden brown liquid. She swallowed. Paused. Just one sip. That's it. Just one.

With a shaky hand, she lifted the plastic bottle to her lips, tipped the bottle and let the liquid joy flow over her lips, down her throat, and into her empty belly. The heat of it exploded in her gut and rushed to her head. She rocked back then steadied herself. Fisting the bottle, her eyes drifted closed as she allowed the warmth to fill her. *Just one more sip. That's it. Just one.*

When Martha awoke it was dark. Her temples pounded. When she tried to sit up, her stomach rebelled. She blinked to get her eyes to adjust to the darkness. *Where was she?* Like puzzle pieces fitting into place, it came back to her bit by bit. She groaned, pressed the heels of her palms into her eyes, and slowly shook her head in shame. *What had she done?* She'd been so good for five long, grueling months. In an instant everything had changed. She didn't want to go back to sleeping on the train or living with countless, nameless faces in a shelter. She had hoped this apartment would be her new beginning, not a headlong dive into the past.

With great effort she pushed up from the bed, not even remembering lying down, and crossed the room toward the bathroom. She turned on the faucets, listened to the bang and clang before the water burst free—not as brown this time. She splashed water on her face, and for some reason, the not-so-brown water felt like a sign—a sign that things were going to get better.

She had no idea what time it was, but she did know the halls and stairs needed to be washed before Mr. Smart had something smart to say. She giggled at her inside joke. Her temples thumped.

Martha closed her eyes and waited for the thumping to stop, but it didn't. And it wasn't in her head. She crossed the room and went to the door. She pressed her ear against the wood.

Thump. Thump. Thump.

Her heart began to race. As quietly as she could, she slipped the chain from the door, turned the knob, and eased the door open.

The man had returned. Methodically, he dragged another suitcase down the stairs, one thumping step at a time.

He must have sensed her. He turned and looked up the staircase and right into her eyes. Martha yelped. There was nothing in his eyes. Nothing. Pure, empty darkness. She felt wetness dribble down her legs.

The man turned away and continued on his downward journey.

Martha shut the door and whimpered like a baby. Never in her life had she been so terrified. But what was most terrifying was that she wasn't certain why she felt terrified.

She waited several moments, long enough, she hoped, for the man with the dark hat and suitcase to be long gone to wherever it was that he went with his load, and then went to the bathroom to clean herself up.

Martha eased open her apartment door and was met with silence. No sounds, no smells. Nothing. She gingerly made her way down the stairs to the ground floor utility closet and took out her supplies.

Mr. Smart's door suddenly opened and sent another jolt of dread coursing through her.

"You're late," he said and shut the door.

Martha swallowed. She gathered her mop, bucket, broom and cleaning agents and trudged back up the stairs. Halfway she stopped. Listened. *A moan?* She shook her head. Must be the aftereffects of the bourbon and the series of frights she'd experienced. She continued up the steps. Stopped. There it was again.

She put down her supplies, stilled her trembling body, and listened again. Nothing. It must be the noise in her head. She was imagining things. *Who would be moaning like that?* She hadn't seen a soul other than the man with the suitcase and Mr. Smart since she'd moved in. But maybe there was someone else living in the building and they were hurt or sick.

The moaning came from 3B.

Martha peeked down and up the staircase. She tiptoed over to 3B but stopped short when she heard footsteps below. As quickly as she could, she gathered her things and continued up the stairs.

Between her pounding head, empty stomach and rattled nerves, it took her three tries before she could fill the bucket with water without sloshing it all over the sink. Her thoughts ran in maddening circles.

She had to tell someone about the strange things happening in the building. *But what would she say that wouldn't make her sound crazy or drunk? Who would believe her if she said there was something sinister about a man who leaves several times a day with a suitcase? Or the landlord wanted her to wash the halls and stairs twice per day? Or there were no sounds or smells in the six-story building? Except that moan.* But now she wasn't sure if she'd heard it or imagined it.

No one would believe her. Instead they would tell her she should consider herself lucky, in the midst of the Great Depression, to have a roof over her head, a room of her own in a quiet building, and all she needed to do to stay there was wash floors.

While she fixed a bologna sandwich, she thought about it all, and she realized how silly she was being. She'd allowed her loneliness to make her think crazy thoughts and do crazy things. *What did she intend to do—go into Apartment 3B? Then what?*

She bit into her sandwich and swore that nothing ever tasted that good. From now on, she was going to do her work and mind her business. She licked her lips and the residue of the bourbon awakened on her tongue. *Come back anytime.*

Martha finished off her sandwich, put on her coat, and tiptoed out and down the stairs. She tried to balance her weight in such a way that the stairs wouldn't creak. The unnamed fear that her presence would somehow disturb the heavy silence plagued her every footfall.

She reached the ground floor without encountering a soul. She took a quick look in the direction of Mr. Smart's door before practically running out of the building.

Martha tugged the collar of her coat close against her throat. The temperature had dipped, and she braced her body against the frosty but still air. She glanced behind her, looked up at 136 Auburn Lane, and squinted at the dimly lit window on the third floor. It was the only light on in the entire building. A man with a hat appeared in the frame of the window. Before he moved out of her line of sight, she swore she saw him drag a limp body across the room.

Martha pressed her fist to her mouth to stifle her cry. Her gaze jumped around the desolate streets. She felt utterly alone. Joe's little corner store was blocks away. It was dark. It was cold. She was afraid. Tears of fear, uncertainty and loneliness dribbled down her cheeks. She clutched her collar tighter as the wind whistled around the corner.

The front door to the building opened. The man with the hat came out dragging a suitcase behind him. Martha got her wits together and scurried around the corner. She pressed her back against the brick wall and held her breath.

With no stairs to bang against, the oversized suitcase took on a new sound—a harsh rustle and scrape of something heavy being dragged over a hard surface.

Martha waited until the sound disappeared. She didn't know where he'd gone or what he was doing. One thing she did know was the man with the hat was the same man she had seen in the window on the third floor, and the third floor was where she'd heard the moans.

She wanted to scream at the top of her lungs, wake up this sleepy hollow neighborhood, and ask people what the hell was happening.

She took a quick peek around the corner. The street had returned to its norm of desolation. Martha turned toward Joe's store silently praying he would be there and let her in. The last thing she wanted to be right then was alone.

When she reached the store, she nearly broke down and wept for the third time that day. She found the shop dark and shuttered as if it hadn't been in operation for years.

She banged on the door. The sound echoed over and over. "Please!" Slowly she slumped into a heap on the icy pavement and curled into a tight ball, hugging her knees to her chest.

When the door creaked open, Martha wasn't sure how long she'd been curled in a knot fighting off her terror and the cold. She lifted her head and blinked against the light that haloed Joe.

"Martha? What'chu doing out here? You gonna freeze to death." He pulled the door all the way open, reached down, and helped her to her feet. "Come on inside."

Next to the bologna sandwich she'd had earlier, this was the best thing to happen to her all day.

Joe pulled out a crate from behind the counter and offered it to her as a seat. He peered at her. "You eat? Hungry?"

Martha sniffed and shuddered from the cold that still clung to her bones. "I could eat something," she managed.

Joe set up a hot plate, made a wobbly tin pot materialize, and filled it with two cans of soup. In short order, the small space was filled with the scent of chicken noodle soup. Martha's stomach yelled.

"Want a little taste?" Joe asked. He held up a bottle of bourbon.

Martha licked her lips. Swallowed. "Uh, no. Thanks." Her fingers trembled and she curled them into fists.

Joe walked away to the back room and returned with a bowl, spoon, and some crackers. He poured the heated soup into the bowl, stuck the spoon in it, and handed the small meal over to Martha.

"Thanks," she mumbled while she wrapped her hands around the warm bowl. She wanted to bring the bowl to her mouth and gulp the contents straight down. She didn't. She took the spoon and took a ladylike sip. Joe tossed the pack of crackers on the third crate he used as a table. The crackers rolled and stopped next to the bottle of bourbon.

Martha's mouth watered. She focused on her soup.

"Want to tell me what you were doing out there?"

She slurped another spoonful of soup. "You wouldn't believe me."

"Why not?"

She looked up from her bowl. Her gaze settled on his impassive expression. "You wouldn't."

Joe shrugged and took a seat on the crate. He poured himself a drink.

"What time is it?" she asked.

Joe took a watch from the inside pocket of his sweater and stared at it briefly. He glanced up. "Nine."

"Um, do you have a phone?"

"Doesn't work. Who do you need to call?"

"A friend." Liz wasn't really a friend, but Joe didn't need to know that. It was best if he thought she had somebody out there who cared about her.

"There's a pay phone about a block away. Can't guarantee that it works."

Martha finished off her soup and then ripped open the package of crackers. "Do...other tenants from 136 ever come in here?"

Joe shrugged. "Don't generally ask where people live," he said, but she didn't believe him. "Why do you want to know?"

"Just asking. Mr. Smart seems to know you."

A muscle in his cheek fluttered. He refilled his glass and tossed back the contents in one gulp.

Martha cleared her throat. "Thank you for the food."

"Sure."

Martha stood.

"Sure you won't have a sip before you go? Fight off the cold out there?" He smiled benevolently and his incisor flashed.

She licked her lips. "Well...maybe just a little."

It was good for Martha that the doors to 136 Auburn were never locked. She would have been unable to find the keyhole with a key. She stumbled through the front doors and giggled to herself.

"Shhh," she said into the cavernous entry as she bobbed and weaved toward the steps that seemed to keep moving away from her. She grabbed hold of the banister and pulled herself up the stairs. What seemed like hours later, she rocked back and forth in front of her apartment door. She smiled at her accomplishment, turned the knob and walked inside, not even bothering to turn on the light. She tugged off her coat and tossed it across the room, stepped out of her shoes, pulled her dress over her head, dropped it on the floor, and collapsed across the narrow bed. The room swam, but she held on tight. Soon she sank into a deep, dreamless sleep.

A scream woke her. She jerked awake. The room was pitch black. Her heart banged in her chest. She tried to make out the shapes within the darkness of her room. There was a riot going on in her head. She must have been dreaming.

Martha flopped back against the paper-thin pillow and closed her eyes. Her mouth felt awful. She needed water but didn't have the energy to get up. Her stomach tumbled. She was going to be sick and she didn't think she would make it to the bathroom.

"No!"

Hair stood up on the back of her neck. She gripped the sheet and stared into the darkness. The room swayed. She blinked, strained to hear. Nothing. *Was she still dreaming? Had she just heard someone scream?*

Martha curled onto her side and brought her knees up to her chin as if she could disappear into a ball. She stayed that way until the sun peeked between her closed lids and pried them open.

The previous night came back to her like scenes from a movie. But there were gaps. She didn't remember how much she'd drunk or how she'd gotten home. She managed to push herself up from the bed and pressed her hands to her temples as if that could somehow keep her head from splitting wide open. Her eyes burned. She stumbled to the bathroom. Stopped. She frowned and tried to force the memory to the surface. Her skin tingled. *Something had frightened her, awakened her. Didn't it?*

Martha stared at her reflection in the dull bathroom mirror. *It was a scream.* Her heart jumped. That's what woke her. She'd heard a scream. Someone screamed 'No!'

But how could she be sure? She'd had so much to drink and she'd been upset. She splashed water on her face, grabbed the towel from the rod, and held it under the water. She washed up as best she could and made a mental note to get soap the next time she went out. *The next time she went out.*

Joe. She'd talked to Joe last night. He gave her soup, and she thought she might have told him about the odd things going on at 136 Auburn. It was the bourbon that had loosened her tongue. But she couldn't be sure. Maybe she only wanted to tell him.

This is why she'd had to stop drinking. Yes, it had caused her to lose her job and then her apartment, but the worst thing was that it made her lose her memory. There were big holes in her memory as if someone had gone in with a shovel and dug parts of it out. As a result, she often couldn't distinguish what was real and what she thought was real. The doctors told her the mind was a tricky beast, and what her mind was doing was finding a way to fill in the gaps, the gaps that were filled with many of her wild imaginings.

The pills helped. They calmed her anxiety, and with no anxiety, the need for a drink was diminished. But she was out of pills, and hell if she wasn't anxious now.

Martha dried her face and then brushed her teeth. After she finished up with her morning chores, she was going to find that pay phone and call Liz. She had no idea what she was going to tell her, but she wanted out. There had to be another halfway house where she could live until she found some kind of work. Whatever was going on at 136 Auburn Lane, she didn't want any part of it.

Martha began her washing and scrubbing. As usual, she didn't see anyone, hear a thing, or smell a scent. All she wanted to do was finish as quickly as her hands and knees would allow so she could call Liz.

She was returning her cleaning supplies to the closet when Mr. Smart stepped out of his apartment. He was dressed in his finest, as usual, and he had on his overcoat.

"All done?"

"Yes." Her skin tingled.

His eyes roved up the stairwell as if to confirm she was telling the truth then settled back on her. "I need you to wait down here in the hallway. I'm expecting a delivery ...of supplies."

"But I...I shouldn't be long. Sign your name for the delivery and let them leave it in front of my door."

Martha swallowed. She wasn't in much of a position to argue. "All right."

Mr. Smart swept passed her and walked out.

Martha watched him go and then sat down on the bottom step to wait.

She must have dozed off. A banging on the front door roused her. She shook her head to clear it. Aching and stiff, she pushed up from the step. Her knee whined in protest as she limped to the front door.

"Delivery for Smart," the man said and shoved a clipboard at her. He handed her a pen.

Martha scrawled her name and returned the clipboard and pen. "You can leave the delivery over there." She pointed toward Mr. Smart's door.

The deliveryman went back to his truck. Moments later he returned with a box at least six feet tall and just as wide. It took several tries for him to get the box into the doorway.

"What's in there?"

"None of my business." He pushed the box off the hand truck and propped it against Mr. Smart's door. He took a look around then his gaze settled on Martha. "Quiet around here, huh?"

Martha swallowed. "Yeah...it is."

"Humph." He turned and walked out.

Martha sighed and then turned her attention to the box. She crossed in front of it several times trying to figure out what could be inside. She tried to push the box to see how heavy it was. It barely moved. She peeked toward the front door to check if anyone was coming. She glanced up the staircase. She went to the utility closet to find something to poke a hole in the box. The best she could find was a broom or mop handle.

She took a broom from the closet, then checked her surroundings again. She got a good grip on the broom handle and shoved it as hard as she could into the side of the box. It made a dent. She went at it again until the head of the handle broke through the box creating a near circular tear.

Martha bent and pushed her eye against the opening but couldn't make out what was inside. She stuck her finger in the hole. Whatever it was it was hard, and smooth like leather. She jerked away.

The sound of thumping echoed from the floor above. *He was coming.* She backed away from the box and returned the broom to the closet. She was shutting the closet door when the man with the hat and the suitcase stopped on the bottom landing.

For an instant he turned and looked at her, yet she couldn't actually see his eyes. Her throat grew dry and she felt like she had to pee.

The man's hidden gaze seemed to slide toward the box. His thin mouth moved, but he didn't say a word. He dragged the hard leather suitcase toward the front door and was gone.

Martha released the breath she only then realized she'd held. Her hands shook. *The box contained suitcases. The same kind of creepy suitcase the man dragged down those damned stairs day after day. What the hell! What was in those suitcases? Where did that man go with the suitcases every day? Where were the other tenants?*

"Hello! Is anybody here?" she screamed. "Hello! Somebody answer me! Pleeeese." Tears rolled down her cheeks.

The front door opened. Martha froze. It was Mr. Smart. Her heart banged in her chest. She swiped at her tears and backed up toward the stairs.

"I see my delivery came." He stared at her with narrowed eyes as if he was trying to see beyond her exterior.

Her throat worked up and down.

He took a set of keys from his pocket and unlocked his apartment door. He pushed and shoved the box inside and shut the door behind him.

Martha slumped against the stairwell. She couldn't stay here. Not a minute longer. She limped as she tried to run up the stairs to her apartment. She had to get in touch with Liz. She would find her some other place to stay. She had to.

Just as she was about to open her apartment door, she heard a sound—a knocking. It was coming from the apartment across the hall. There it was again as if someone was...she didn't know. She took a quick look down the staircase and then tiptoed toward the knocking sound.

There it was again.

Martha pressed her ear to the door. "Hello," she whispered.

Footsteps on the stairs—coming up.

Martha scurried across the hall to her apartment and ducked inside. She pressed her eye to the keyhole. Moments later the man with the hat appeared at the top of the stairs. He had a suitcase, apparently light enough to carry since she hadn't heard the usual thumping.

He used a key, opened the apartment door, and shut it behind him. Martha's heart was hammering so hard she felt it hitting against her door.

Christ almighty. What was she going to do? She spun around in a slow circle as if looking for a place to escape. There was nowhere to go, but she no longer cared. She was leaving. Tonight. She was going to pack her things, walk out the front door, and never look back. Whatever the hell was going on in this godforsaken place, she didn't want any part of it. She hurried across the room and tossed her few belongings into a bag and then went to the make-believe kitchen and gathered up what was left of the food. She stuffed the food in her bag as well. That's when she noticed the half bottle of bourbon on the side of the bed.

Martha licked her lips. Her temples pounded. She took a step toward the bottle, bent down and picked it up. *How had it gotten there?* She didn't remember bringing it home from the store. Sure she had a lot to drink the night before and she remembered coming home pretty wasted. What she didn't remember was bringing home a half bottle of bourbon. She turned the bottle around in her hands. She swallowed and her throat was suddenly dry. Maybe just a little taste, that's all. She took a look around as if someone might be watching before she brought the bottle to her lips.

The warmth flowed through her veins like a transfusion. She stepped back and sat down on the side of the bed. There was a buzzing sound, electric. She dismissed it as the buzz going on in her head. She stared at the bottle. Just one more. She brought it to her lips and took a savoring swallow.

Thump.

Martha jumped up, sloshing some of the contents of the bottle down the front of her dress. There it was again. She didn't even want to say out loud the images of terror that ran through her head: a lone man, countless suitcases that go up empty and come down full. *Full of what?* The answer was too impossible, too horrid to be true.

She scurried over to the door and peeked through the peephole. The hallway stood empty and the rhythmic thud of the suitcase bumping against the stairs grew faint. Her bottom lip trembled and she blinked back tears.

It was nothing more than her imagination, her hunger and the liquor playing tricks with her mind, she told herself. She risked opening the door.

Her scream clung to the back of her throat. A thin stream of urine ran down her leg as she came face to face with Mr. Smart.

"Going somewhere?" He looked past her to the bag on the bed.

"I...um." She swallowed.

Mr. Smart crossed the threshold and walked to the center of the room. He turned to face her. "Well?"

"I was just straightening up, that's all."

"Hmm. Well, don't let the time slip away. You have work to do." He took a step toward her. "We have a way of doing things here, Martha, and if you intend to keep a roof over your head, I suggest you follow the rules. There are plenty of people out there who would love to be in your place."

She couldn't imagine who they would be if they knew what she knew, or thought what she thought. "I'm sure you're right."

"Do what you came here to do, and we won't have any problems. I'd hate for us to have any problems. This home serves a purpose to those unfortunate souls who have been hit hard by this awful depression." His gold incisor blinked at her. "I'm sure you understand that our work must continue, and you are a vital part of that work."

Martha blinked back tears. "Of course."

"Have a good day." He walked to the door.

"Where are all of the other tenants?" she blurted out.

Mr. Smart's hand gripped the doorknob. He glanced at her over her shoulder.

"Everyone is where they are supposed to be."

Martha swallowed.

Mr. Smart turned the knob and opened the door. "It's getting late." He closed the door behind him.

Martha collapsed in a heap right in the middle of the floor. She wasn't sure how long she sat there, frozen, but finally she pulled herself up and stood on shaky legs. It wasn't her imagination or her drinking. Something awful was happening in this building. She had to tell someone.

After cleaning herself up and changing into her other dress and pair of panties, she sat on the side of the bed, grabbed the bottle, and tipped it to her lips. The booze went down easy, fortifying her and clouding her dark thoughts.

Slowly she pushed to her feet. She swayed for a moment and chuckled to herself about how silly she was being. She went downstairs to begin her chores. The building hummed with its usual deathly silence. The only sounds were her labored breathing, her intermittent laughter, and the swish of the mop across the floors.

When she was done and had returned her supplies to the utility closet on the main floor, she stopped in front of Mr. Smart's apartment. Feeling bold, she pressed her ear to the door and then knocked. She waited. He didn't answer. She looked behind her and then tried the knob. She gasped when the door opened. She stuck her head in.

"Hello! Mr. Smart. I'm all done." Her heart banged in her chest. She stepped in. "Mr. Smart?"

She could barely see into the dim interior. The curtains were drawn, but she could make out stacks and stacks of oversized suitcases piled against the walls. She inched further inside.

In the center of the oppressive space sat a worn wooden desk piled high with paper. She walked to it, picked up the first sheet of paper, and squinted in the dark to make out what was typed on it. It looked like a list of names. Pages and pages of names, and each one had a line drawn through it and a date next to the name. *Crossed out.*

Her temples pounded. She blinked and looked again at the list of names. Martha Hopewell. There was a date next to her name. December 21, 1932. Two days from now. It was all she could do to keep the scream from racing up from her throat. Whatever bit of elation the liquor had provided was gone. She dropped the paper as if it had suddenly caught fire and began backing up toward the door. That's when she noticed the wall of photographs. Hundreds of pictures were tacked to the wall. She inched closer to get a better look.

There were several faces she recognized, all of them from The Center. All of them had X's across their faces. When she spotted her own image the yelp she'd held onto escaped. She stumbled backward, knocking over a stack of suitcases. The noise, to her, sounded like an explosion. She ran to the door and smack into Mr. Smart.

"Martha, this is very unfortunate." He shut the door behind him.

Martha kept backing up until she bumped into the desk. Frantically she looked around in the dullness of the room for a way out.

"If only you would have done as you were told." He took a step toward her. "The streets are littered with countless unfortunate souls like yourself because of this awful depression. But we here on Auburn Lane have been charged with cleaning up the streets. Without the heavy weight the homeless and jobless pose to society, we can recover. You do understand, don't you?"

She held her hands up, palms facing him. "Please..."

He pushed out a resigned breath and slowly shook his head. "I tried to tell Liz we have to move faster."

"Liz?" she squeaked as the pieces of the unimaginable fully took shape in her head. Liz was sending homeless and jobless folks like her here all under the guise of providing them with a place of their own—only to wind up in a suitcase. *Who could she turn to now? Who would believe a homeless, on-again off-again drinker?*

Mr. Smart turned the lock on the door and then took another step toward her.

"I'll scream!"

Mr. Smart laughed. "Who is going to hear you?"

Martha kept her eyes on him while she reached behind her, her hand frantically feeling for something. Anything. She found something square and heavy.

Mr. Smart took his hands out of his pockets. He took two quick steps and he was on her.

◆ ◆ ◆

Two months later, Sue Grimshaw dragged her tattered suitcase up the hill of Auburn Lane. She dug in her coat pocket to check the slip of paper Liz at The Center had given her. 136 Auburn Lane. Apt. 1A. The building was at the top of the hill positioned halfway between Harlem and the Bronx.

Funny, she thought as she lugged her suitcase, there wasn't a soul on the street. The silence sounded deafening. If that was possible. At this point Sue didn't care. All she cared about was having a room of her own, and a little job to pay for her keep. She'd been at the shelter for six months, and it was finally her turn to move on. She felt grateful to Liz for picking her out of the hundreds who lined the single beds at night to give her a second chance.

Sue stood in front of the six-story building and looked up at the darkened windows. A momentary sense of unease fluttered in her stomach. She glanced behind her. No one. Drawing in a deep breath, she walked up the pathway to the front door and was surprised to find it unlocked. She walked in.

The cavernous entryway echoed with her footfalls. The quiet was overwhelming until she heard a thumping sound that seemed to be coming down the stairs. A man in a dark fedora pulling an oversized suitcase appeared at the top of the stairs. He paused a moment when he spotted her before he continued down.

"Hell—o," she said tentatively when the man was nearly in front of her.

He barely glanced in her direction, walked past her, and out.

"Rude!" She huffed and crossed the entryway and up to 1A. She knocked on the door.

Moments later the door opened.

"Hello, My name is Sue Grimshaw. Liz sent me over."

"Of course. Welcome. I'm Martha Hopewell. I'll show you to your room. I'm sure you're exhausted and want to get settled." She stepped out the apartment and shut the door. "Follow me."

"Thank you so much. This place is a godsend. Things are really rough out there. I'm just happy to get a chance to rebuild my life," Sue said.

Martha looked over her shoulder and flashed a benevolent smile at her guest. "We all have to do what we must to survive."

Now that you have finished *Approaching Footsteps*,
please consider leaving it an honest review on Amazon,
Goodreads, Litsy and/or your favorite book apps and blogs.
Reviews are the most direct and concrete way to help these
authors and flash fiction writers reach new readers.

Thank you!

SPECIAL READER'S BONUS

Flash Fiction by the Winners and Judges
of the Spider's Web Flash Fiction Prizes

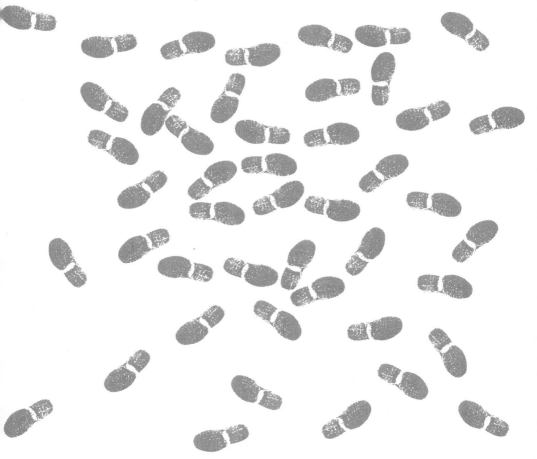

BRIGIDA

Kate Spitzmiller

2015 First Place Winner

THE LAST TIME I SAW my husband Marcus, he was heading north out of Eboracum with the legion. The morning sunlight glinted off his bronze helmet, and the red horsehair crest standing up from the crown waved in Britannia's cold autumn wind.

My husband was a centurion, in charge of a hundred men. His legion, the Ninth, was headed for Caledonia. My husband, and the legion, never returned.

Six thousand men. Gone.

There were rumors. Rumors that the Scots of Caledonia had annihilated them, devoured their lines like the ancient giant Cacus who had consumed live human flesh and displayed human heads on nails outside his cave on the Palatine Hill.

I did not know what happened to the legion. Nor did I want to know.

All I knew was that I was alone.

I was not Roman. I was Brigante—native to this occupied land—and only partially accepted by my husband's cohorts because of his status as an officer. And now I was a Brigante alone in a Roman city. I could not go home, across the green hills to my small Brigante village. Falling in love with a Roman soldier had sealed my fate as an outsider. No Brigante would ever open their door to me again, not my mother or my father, and not my brothers.

I heard that the wives of the officers were receiving money—10,000 denarii per month. So I walked through the cobbled streets to the legion headquarters to speak with the treasurer. There was a long line of Roman wives, and I waited with them, bundled in our woolen cloaks against the bitter autumn wind. Winter would be coming soon to Eboracum.

When it was my turn to speak with the treasurer—a balding, bored-looking man in a dark brown cloak—I spoke in my halting Latin, asking about my denarii.

He narrowed his eyes. "What is your name?" he said.

"Brigida."

"That is not a Roman name."

"I am wife to Marcus Quintus Flavius, Centurion of the Ninth Legion."

"From where do you get your accent?"

"I am Brigante."

"There is no denarii for you here. Only Roman wives receive payment."

I thought perhaps I misunderstood him with my weak Latin.

"My husband," I said. "He is a centurion."

"Go," the treasurer said, waving his hand. "There is nothing for you here."

As I turned and walked past the line of Roman wives who stood waiting for their denarii, I heard their whispers, heard their snickering.

I walked back toward our quarters, a small, three-room villa beside the west wall of the city. The wind had risen, and I pulled my cloak up around my neck.

There is nothing for you here.

Marcus had left me his signet ring. He had given me instructions. Were anything to ever happen to him, I was to go to Rome, to his father's house on the Tiber. There I was to show Marcus' ring. I would be taken in, Marcus had said, taken care of. We never discussed how I would get to Rome, only that I would go. Marcus had me swear an oath to him, promising, and so I had.

I packed a leather bag with three loaves of hard wheat bread and a satchel of beans, and I packed my two wool *pallas*, shawls to be worn under my cloak when winter came. I searched Marcus' belongings and found a flint striker for starting fires, wool leggings, and a sharp knife. Those, too, went into my leather bag.

I did not know the way to Rome. I only knew it lay far to the south of Britannia—past Gaul, past Germania, on a peninsula surrounded by a great wide sea. And I knew I had made a promise to my Marcus, and there was nothing left for me in Eboracum.

The day I chose to leave was cold and bright. It was early morning, and frost clung to the grasses that lined the deserted streets as I walked alone to the south gate. A small bird, a finch perhaps, whistled from an oak tree as I passed. The smell of hearth fires burning filled the air. The city was waking.

The soldiers at the south gate looked bored. They barely glanced at me as I passed through, leaving Eboracum, leaving my life with Marcus, for good.

And then the road was before me, straight and true.

The road to Rome.

CRAZY JEN

Helen Angove

2015 Second Place Winner

IN THE EYES OF US, the new officer intake, she was a technological fossil. She unnerved us with her pitted and scarred hull, so different from the slick, streamlined vessels on which we had trained. But we were also reassured by her evident ability to survive. We laughed at her in the messroom when we were all together and the beer was flowing, but I suspect many of us, when we were alone in our cribs, were also soothed to sleep by the lullaby of her engines.

There was one repair that intrigued me—a brownish, organic-looking excrescence on the interior of the hull, down in the cargo hold. It was a little over half a meter long and looked oily to the touch, but its surface was actually cool and hard and slightly transparent, revealing murky shapes within. But it was not so much the repair itself that fascinated me, as the behavior of one of the crew around it.

Crazy one-armed Jen had been on the ship far longer than any of the rest of us. Her face was a hotchpotch of broken veins and ugly, blackened lesions, and she had long, white hair and distorted, emaciated limbs. Zero-g does that to you, if you're exposed to it long enough. I wondered how come she hadn't been invalided home long ago.

I sometimes saw Crazy Jen down there in the hold, brooding over the repair. She didn't seem to do much—just touched it occasionally, as if to reassure herself it was still there. Once when she thought no one was looking, I noticed her run her hand along the length of it in a manner almost like a caress.

The officer's mess was closed one night, so I was in the regular messroom having a beer, and seeing Jen close by, I remembered my question. A momentary lull in the raucous bawdiness gave me a chance to pose it.

Jen leered and grasped a grab bar to pull herself closer. Her hair undulated around her face. "Buy us a beer, and I'll tell you.

"It was nearly thirty years ago when I first come on board this ship. She was new then, one of the first they built. None of these fancy safety features then, force fields and the like, but they built her to last. That's why they never decommissioned her, see? Cheaper to just keep on repairing.

"Anyway, it was the darnedest thing. I was down in the hold doing repairs, and there was this almighty bang. Out the corner of my eye I saw something tiny whiz across the room.

"Ship's engineer said later it was the strangest thing he'd ever seen. Meteoroid hit a weak spot at just the right angle and just the right speed to make this little hole in the hull—no bigger than a penny. Then, the other side of the hold, it hit a bulkhead and stopped it from going right through. Biggest fluke you ever saw, but then if it'd happened any other way, I wouldn't be here telling you this now.

"Straight off I could hear the air escaping. No time to think. I just slammed me arm against the hole and started praying.

"The doc said if I hadn't been wearing my regulation overalls, I'd have been done for. Seems that bit of fancy fabric protected my skin just enough to seal off the hole. Didn't stop the cold, though. By the time they found me, I was half dead from hypothermia and asphyxiation.

"Well, they got the doc down there, and the engineers, and they tried to decide what to do. See, the arm was pretty well gone through frostbite an' radiation anyway, and they didn't want to risk moving it 'cos they didn't know if the integrity of the hull could take it. So in the end, they just lopped me arm off at the elbow, covered it with resin, and left it there.

"Funny thing is, I can still feel that arm, even though I lost it so long ago. Sometimes it itches like you wouldn't believe, and the only thing I can do is go on down to the hold and scratch it. They all think I'm crazy.

"That's why they never pensioned me off. Maybe I'd have liked to go back to earth, settled down, had kids, but I couldn't leave me arm behind."

WHEN I WORE PINK BOOTS

Holly Walrath

2015 Third Place Winner

ONCE I HAD NO FEAR. Like little kids do. Oh, they smell fear, they can taste it in the air, but they do not feel it themselves.

There was a moment when I had no fear, a moment in the sun and light and dust in the Texas summer. The heat was against me that day, but I had no fear. I was getting on that horse, and that's all there was to it. A moment capsulated in my memory like those bugs in amber from primeval times. Yes, this is an early memory.

There are no faces, only the heat, and the way it wavered over the dirt— red-brown dirt—that never seemed to settle, in a corral with white cowboy fences bleached with age and sun and dust, the sound of the horse gasping heavy short bursts, panting, and the sound of the hooves pawing in the dust. I could feel—smell—the fear and sweat on its body, so brown and tense, straining against the reins, its handler off to the side not seeing it sway. Tired, tired, its hairs expanded, standing up along its back and tail flicked, swishing like a clock hand in a steady rhythm.

My feet were planted on the fence. I placed my hand on the saddle horn and gripped it. I put my boot in the strap, and then the familiar sensation of rising into the saddle, the way the leather creaked underneath my hands, my body light and tense and sinuous all at once, and then—the clatter, the tumult all around me as the horse reared, and I was sliding like an avalanche.

Yes, I was going to fall, and there was nothing to be done about it. No one to catch me, no hands to steady the beast, no way for me to escape injury—death.

I was not afraid, although I could feel its fear. I did not hear the screams or scrambling feet, but only felt its clawing paws in the air and the poor thing's heart pounding beneath me, trembling. I needed to get away, to be free, to step off the edge—to save myself—like every jumper who thinks the end is their deliverance and the feeling of the air rushing through them will only be a moment and then sweet release, sweet redemption.

My eyes were so clear, hazel green-brown, reflective of the cedar trees and dry grass on the horizon. My thoughts were so clear, knowing what to do. I simply

jumped

off

the horse.

THOMAS

Melissa Algood

Honorable Mention

SOMETIMES I DREAM of my hypothetical son.

He'll jump on the bed, wake his dad and me proclaiming it's his sixth birthday. I'll brush his dark brown hair from his forehead, kiss his cheeks with skin that turns a perfect caramel color when he's been out in the sun too long, and thank him for reminding me.

He will miraculously appear that very morning.

I'll make him a chocolate cake, from scratch, then pipe 'Thomas' in robin's egg blue icing. As it cools, my son and his dad will play a game of catch in the backyard. Afterwards our son will run his sweaty finger along the side of the bright white mixing bowl, and he'll giggle as he licks it clean.

We'll take him bowling, where he'll score a 300, and the whole alley will sing 'Happy Birthday' to my son right before he blows out the candles on his cake.

There will be water balloon fights, which his Dad will win, then my son and I will turn the garden hose on him. My son will gaze in wonderment as a rainbow stretches across the yard. He'll run through the rush of lukewarm water in an attempt to catch it, and refuse to come inside until the sun goes down. When we tuck him in to sleep, I'll stay and read to him about the greatest teenage wizard in all of England.

"Is there really magic, Mommy?" he'll ask.

I'll grin, and whisper to him, making it a secret between us. "Yes, Thomas. That's how you got here.

When he gets the flu, I'll sleep with him every night in the hopes the virus will use me as its host, and not my beloved.

He'll hold my hand when we're out in public, and ask me to hold on tighter if we come across a snake. The cold, slimy, slithering reptiles will be his only fear.

Then one day he won't intertwine my fingers with his. He won't ask me to kiss his scraped knees from climbing every tree on the block. His body will stretch, as if made of taffy, and not every wish I ever had. There will be no time for enunciation, only mumbling. My son's clothing won't be neon colored and mismatched anymore, but dark and oversize. He'll only want to talk to me if he needs money or advice about a girl.

I'll gaze at my son, the most perfect creature to grace planet Earth. Although I'll know that no girl will be worthy to breathe the same air, I'll say, "Treat her with respect, ask her questions, and make sure to meet her parents before you take her out."

He'll grunt at me, and I'll throw an arm around him for one last embrace before he's completely lost to me. He'll reciprocate, if only for a moment, and I'll savor every millisecond of it. Then before he leaves the room, I'll call out to his slouched frame, "And for God's sake, use a condom, Tom."

I'll blink.

And when I open my eyes, I will be at his wedding. She'll claim to love him forever and a day. I'll scoff because no one will love him more than I—the woman that created him with her thoughts alone.

Then, he'll be gone.

My son will call and tell me he's graduated law school and medical school. He'll travel the world with his wife and twin girls who will help him brush up on the five languages he's fluent in.

He'll return when my eyes are milky, skin tattered as crumpled wet newsprint, and a mind that has dulled like the crayons he used to draw with. I'll beg him to let me die in my own bed, like his dad did years prior. This time he'll be the one sleeping next to me, wrapping his long, muscular arms around a shrunken, shivering woman who had once been so strong. He'll remind me of the wizard's mentor who said we shouldn't fear death. He'll tell me I did everything right, and he only became the man he is because of me.

My ashes will be spread in the Atlantic Ocean, but no one will miss me. There will only be tears for Thomas, the greatest man who will ever live. The man who mysteriously faded into nothingness, because he existed only in my dreams.

BECAUSE THE SKY IS BLUE

Andrea Barbosa

Honorable Mention

LANA PICKED UP the broken pieces of crayons she had collected from under the tables when she was cleaning the restaurant and spread them on her bedroom floor. A white piece of cardboard was ready to be used as the canvas for her next masterpiece.

"What do you do with these crayons?" She recalled a customer asking her. She had no idea she was being observed. The gentleman came to the restaurant often with his wife and two children. She had heard the waitresses mention he gave great tips because he was the president of some company and traveled a lot.

"I...I like to draw," she had answered, a bit embarrassed by the unexpected contact with a customer. The janitorial staff was usually invisible and had no business interacting with patrons.

"What do you draw?" The man had insisted on the conversation.

Lana had dug inside her jeans pocket and pulled out a crumpled piece of paper. She showed it to the customer. The beautiful picture of Burj Al Arab resembling a sail boat in the middle of an island revealed itself.

"You draw places you want to travel to?" he had asked.

"Yes. One day I'll travel. As sure as the sky is blue..."

"Dream, because the sky is blue," she heard him say.

Lana looked around her small bedroom with no windows. The walls were covered in the beautiful, colorful drawings she had made with the broken pieces of crayons, depicting cities she longed to visit: Paris, London, Venice, New York, even Athens. "One day, I'll pack and go, because the sky is blue," she thought while coloring different hues of a blue sky on her makeshift canvas as the background for her own Burj Al Arab.

◆ ◆ ◆

"It was an accident. I'm so sorry." Lana apologized while picking up the broken pieces of dinner plates peppering the floor of the restaurant. Waitresses were leading the customers away from the hazard. She was mortified, even more so because it happened in front of the only customer who had ever shown interest in her as a person—someone who hadn't made fun of her dreams.

"Didn't I tell you not to enter the dining room during busy hours?" The manager yelled at her with a menacing look. "What the hell happened?"

"I tripped over the broom when she was sweeping," the waiter said in a shaky voice. He couldn't believe he had dropped the dishes on the floor. Lana didn't want to look up. She continued to clean the mess she had caused while tears streamed down her face.

"You're fired," the manager said to her. "Finish cleaning this up and get the hell out. I don't want to see your face around here no more."

Lana marveled at the enchanting view. Like magic, the Burj Al Arab with its entire splendor seemed to be sailing by her bedroom window. She reached inside her purse and picked up the crumpled picture of the Burj Al Arab she had shown to a customer five years ago, just a few days before the fatalistic day she was fired from the restaurant. She opened her suitcase and took out the old cardboard canvases that had decorated the walls of her barren bedroom. They all had red checkmarks on them. She found her drawing of Dubai and painted a red checkmark on it.

"How do you like it?" the comforting, familiar voice asked her.

"I'm amazed! I can't wait to have the children draw this, looking at the real model!"

"I believe they're ready to do it," he said. His two children ran inside the room in excitement. "You're the best art teacher. I'm so glad you accepted the offer to work for us."

Lana smiled and hugged the children. She looked out the window again and whispered to herself the words she heard from him long ago.

"Dream, because the sky is blue."

PLEIKU, 1969

Kate Spitzmiller

Honorable Mention

THE WHUMP, WHUMP, WHUMP of helicopter blades cut through the humid night air. My stomach twisted, as usual. And as usual, I took a deep breath and whispered, "Steady, Lynch, steady."

I stood in the doorway of the 71st Evac Hospital, my surgical gown whipped by the tornado riled up by the rotors of the two choppers landing on our double pad. The red running lights of the choppers coming in behind them glowed in the darkness beyond, growing closer, like dragons swooping in, threatening to consume us.

The chaos of rolling gurneys and shouting medics and screaming men began. I was assigned to the last chopper, the fourth one, and so I waited, the bleeding and burnt bodies rolling past me one after the other, until the first two dust-offs had unloaded and taken off, sending Pleiku's red dust swirling.

I ran for my chopper as it was landing, followed by a mini-brigade of medics pushing gurneys. I leaned inside and surveyed the damage.

Four litters.

No screaming. This was either very bad or very good.

My medics hauled the litters off the steel shelves they had been shoved onto out in the boonies, and I began my triage. Belly. Shoulder. Partial leg amputation. Bad head wound. Not good.

I pointed to each in turn, shouting out to the medics which soldier should go where—the belly and leg to surgery, the shoulder to the ward, and the head wound to expectants. Bad head wounds nearly always went to expectants. They were the ones we didn't have the capacity to save at the 71st. They were the ones we expected to die.

I followed behind my expectant and got caught up in the mob of gurneys piled up in the doorway of the ER. There wasn't enough room inside for all the wounded.

I gripped the gurney's side rail and shouted across the chaos to the head nurse. "Ruth! We gotta make room!"

"Trying, Cassie!"

Something touched my hand. My expectant had laid his fingers across my knuckles.

He spoke. "Cassie? Cassie Lynch?"

Small bumps rose on the skin of my arms.

I leaned down. His face was a bloody wreck. The side of his head was caved in.

"Yeah," I said. "I'm Cassie."

"It's Billy. From Roosevelt High. Class of '64."

Billy. Did I know a Billy?

I took his hand. "Hey, Billy."

"Do you remember that poem you wrote? The one Mr. Porter had you read to us in English class?"

I didn't remember.

"Sure, Billy, I remember."

"I really liked that poem."

He shifted his head. A beige blob slid out from behind his ear.

Brain matter.

"Try not to move too much," I said.

"Could you recite that poem for me, Cassie? I'd sure like to hear it again."

I had no idea what he was talking about.

"Sure, Billy."

All I could remember was a poem I'd memorized for English Lit class senior year. And I didn't know all of it.

I squeezed his hand. *"If I should die, think only this of me; that there's some corner of a foreign field that is forever England."*

"That's nice," he said.

"Cass!" Ruth yelled.

"Yeah!"

"We've got room for expectants! Everyone else has to wait!"

I pushed Billy into the madness of the ER. The smell of blood and urine hung in the air. Men screamed, nurses shouted, and blood covered the floor—a normal night for us, hell on earth for the wounded.

The place where the healing happened was straight ahead through double doors to surgery, but Billy and I went left instead, to the expectant room. The small room was nearly full. Some men groaned, others were silent. Some were probably already dead. I found Billy a spot in the corner.

"It's nice here," he said. "Quiet." More beige globs had oozed onto his sheet. "Can you finish the poem?"

"Sure, Billy." I took his hand. "But I only remember the end."

He was silent.

I squeezed his hand. *"A body of England's breathing English air...blest by the suns of home."*

"Cass!" Ruth stood in the doorway. "Hancock needs you in surgery!"

Billy's hand was limp in mine. I touched my fingers to his wrist, feeling for a pulse. Nothing.

"Now, Cass."

I squeezed Billy's hand again and placed it gently on his chest, just above his heart. And then I turned my back to him—and to all the others—and left the room.

KIT-CAT CLOCK

Patricia Flaherty Pagan

2015 Judge

LIKE I TELL MY DAUGHTER, nobody saves you. Nobody can. You have to be your own ally.

The wide-eyed Kit-Cat clock on the wall smiled down that Monday night, the only witness. The cat saw the mouse-quiet way The Bastard pretended to look at candles in the back until Sylvia, a regular, left. I listened to the wind hissing against the front windows. But the cat caught the beady eyes under The Bastard's greasy Red Sox cap.

The Bastard came at me in the front of the store. He grabbed my left wrist. While I leaned towards the counter, trying to slam my right hand down on the red alarm button next to the register, The Bastard made a fist and clocked me good on the right side of the head. Sounds got muffled. Warm blood trickled out of my right ear. Then he crashed me onto the floor.

I tried to claw him off the buttons of my jeans, but his gloved hands swatted mine away. He pinned both of my arms back. Then I bit my lip and waited. The Bastard couldn't go on forever. The cat watched. I focused on not thinking about skin on skin and concentrated on the gray opposite of thinking. Meanwhile, the cat's small, white second hand twitched.

Eventually, The Bastard rolled off me, stood, jimmied the register open, emptied the cash drawer, and took off. The cat saw me gather up my jeans and pull myself up to stand. Drops of blood and sperm dripped down the sides of my inner thighs. Time shifted. My legs refused to work. Wrapped in the cloud of The Bastard's musky stink, I froze there for maybe five, or maybe thirty-five, minutes. Then I dragged myself out, drove home in my Chevy, and showered him off of me.

The next day, Detective Virginia Dubois brought me a Styrofoam cup of weak coffee. Could I identify him? The lack of physical evidence would cost me. She couldn't make any promises.

Driving home, I wondered what cops promised the ponytailed UNH girls, the moms with Lego pieces in their pockets, the librarians carrying *The Norton*

Anthology of Nice. As the PTA types whispered, I'd been around. Not a lot of single, white moms with brown-skinned babies north of Manchester. Three consecutive stoner poets had been in and out of my one-bedroom before they went back on the road. A leather skirt and a bad-girl-with-a-heart-of-gold wink kept my landlord amused and my rent under nine hundred a month but hadn't won me any friends.

Never heard back from Virginia.

With a kid at home, I had to be practical. Two Monday nights later, I went back to work with an old Swiss Army Knife in the pocket of my new, Goodwill Levi's. The wide-eyed Kit-Cat clock on the wall smiled down, the only witness. At closing time, I pulled the cat down and smashed it. I didn't need a witness.

Nobody saves you. Nobody can. You have to be your own ally.

PARCEL POST

Eden Royce

2016 Judge

THERE ARE NO signs for Walton.

The town or village or hamlet—whatever it called itself—was impossible to find if you didn't already live there. Of course, you could stop a pleasant-looking stranger on the street for directions. But upon hearing Walton, his face would freeze, its welcoming smile intact, and he would step backward a pace, subconsciously wanting to increase his distance. He would mutter something unintelligible as an excuse. As he left you there on the sidewalk, he'd wish you luck, not in finding your destination, but in hoping you'd give up and never locate the place. He'd go to bed that night soothing himself with thoughts that he'd saved you—perhaps himself as well—from damage.

Camille, however, found Walton without difficulty. One final parcel remained in her bag. One delivery and she would be finished for the day. Her messenger bag flopped against her side, empty now. The one package was marked *Fragile* and *Keep This Side Up*, and she held it in her hands as she scoured Carrelldon Street looking for 101.

She was at eighty-nine when she heard footsteps behind her. She glanced over her shoulder, but saw nothing. No cars parked along the street. No voices. Still. Strange. The wind stirred, pushing against her back enough to hurry her steps forward. Shaking her head at her lively imagination, she continued up the road.

Ninety-two.

Ninety-four.

The wind stopped. Footsteps again.

Camille picked up her pace, her cross-trainers crunching the fine layer of sand on the sidewalk. She was nervous now. Sweating. Not willing to turn around. Deliver the package.

Fragile.

The package was most important. No, it was her. Her safety. Her life.

Ninety-eight.

Steps behind closer. *Don't look.*

Keep This End Up.

She scurried with the package pressed against her breasts.

Don't run.

Camille forced herself to breathe, drag air in and push it out. Heart thudding, it drowned out the sound of her increased breathing. Her breathing drowned out the sound of the footsteps. But she knew they were there. Somewhere. She had pepper spray if she needed it. Somewhere.

One-oh-one.

Breathe deep. Relax. Calm yourself.

The steps were no longer behind her. They were alongside and she gasped with shock. With fright. A scrabble of rough hands and fingers. The package yanked from her grasp.

A hooded man—was it a man?—ran away from her down Carrelldon Street in Walton, a place she'd never delivered to before. Not in seven years.

Camille didn't pursue as the thief ran. She counted the stately houses as he—possibly a he—pounded past them.

One-oh-five. Oh-seven.

The explosion came as he reached 109. Heat and sand pelted the back of her neck and her calves as she turned away from the blast. She heard nothing after the echo of the boom, after the ringing in her ears ebbed away. Still. Strange.

Camille pulled out her work tablet and uploaded a document to complete and send to the company. Under "Location of Incident," she typed *Walton.*

FUZZY DICE

Kathryn Kulpa

2016 Judge

I'M SITTING IN MY CAR outside school, waiting for the right time to go in. Not too early because Sean might be waiting near the doors, or Andie might be hanging around the lockers. Not too late because I can't afford another demerit. I take a pencil from my purse and jab it into that sweet spot on my upper thigh. I told myself I'd stop after last time when it got infected, and I looked down at my jeans during homeroom and saw a dark patch of blood. I wore my big hoodie all day and nobody said anything. That night I poured tons of hydrogen peroxide on it and promised God I'd stop. When I said the word GOD in my head, I saw it printed out in big red letters, only reversed, so it said DOG, and I decided my dog, Hermione, was going to be my conscience, like Jiminy Cricket was for Pinocchio.

"Hermione, you really are the brightest dog of your age," we say to her as a joke because she's actually not very bright, but she knows guilt when she smells it.

Hermione sat with me while I was doing homework and seemed to look at me sadly, as if she was disappointed every time I pulled that pencil out, so I stopped for a while. I did use the safety pin on my arm, but the safety pin is so tiny, you can barely see the blood.

When Andie and I were little kids, we did the pin-prick thing with our pinky fingers. "Let this red blood flow together, make us sisters now and ever!" These days I try not to look at her, and when we talk, I make sure it's shallow talk, homework and movies and funny dog memes.

I watch the fuzzy dice hanging from my mirror. Sean gave them to me last year when we were in *Grease* together. I can't imagine ever being that person again, trying out for a show, letting people watch me and judge me. Sean doesn't understand why I've changed. He's the same person he's always been.

Except maybe a little sadder now. He doesn't know why I broke up with him, why I dodge him in school, don't answer his texts. I don't want to see Sean or Andie or anyone else who used to know the girl who used to be me.

So I avoid. Avoidance is a wonderful thing, and I've learned to do it so well. If I avoid Sean long enough, he'll stop asking why and start believing the version I put out—that we just drifted apart.

If I quit drama. If I stop going to Honor Society meetings. If I say no to parties, sleepovers, movies, the mall. If I lose my phone.

I drain the last of my coffee, watch the black dots on the fuzzy green dice until the dots blur into each other. Five dots. Five quick jabs—I have time for that.

And then I look up and Andie is there, number two on my top-ten list of people I don't want to see. She's holding out a coffee, so I hold mine up to show her I've already got one. I open the door. Andie tells me to shut it. She gets in next to me. She takes my arm, the one with five tiny pinprick spots. "I have to talk to you."

She's known Sean longer than I have. They're neighbors. Maybe he put her up to this. But I can't tell her any more than I could tell Sean.

It's not Sean's fault his father's a pig. I should have known. I shouldn't have let him take me home that time. But Andie doesn't need to know that. Her mom's going through chemo. She doesn't need my problems.

Then there's my mom. I've started hearing her laugh again lately, for the first time since Dad left. And Sean's mom, of course. And his sister. So many lives to ruin.

"Don't tell," he whispered. So I won't tell. I'll etch it into my skin if I have to, letter by letter, word by word.

I try to pull away from Andie, but she won't let go. She tells me about Sean's sister who's hanging out at Andie's all the time now, like she's afraid to go home.

Sean's sister. She's twelve.

All I want is to jab something sharp into myself, sharp enough I won't feel anything but that pain. I look at the dots on the dice, spreading and blurring. If I cry, I'll have to tell Andie everything. And I feel the tears come.

CONTRIBUTORS

RITA BANERJEE

RITA BANERJEE is the Executive Director of Kundiman, the Creative Director of the Cambridge Writers' Workshop, and a Visiting Professor of Creative Writing at Fordham University. She received her doctorate in Comparative Literature from Harvard and her MFA in Creative Writing from the University of Washington, and her writing appears in *The Rumpus, Los Angeles Review of Books, Electric Literature, VIDA: Women in Literary Arts, AWP WC&C Quarterly, Queen Mob's Tea House, Riot Grrrl Magazine, The Fiction Project, Objet d'Art*, KBOO Radio's *APA Compass*, and elsewhere. Her first collection of poems, *Cracklers at Night* (Finishing Line Press), received First Honorable Mention for Best Poetry Book of 2011-2012 at the Los Angeles Book Festival, and her novella, *A Night with Kali* (Spider Road Press), is forthcoming in October 2016. A finalist for the 2015 Red Hen Press Benjamin Saltman Award and the 2016 Aquarius Press Willow Books Literature Award, she is currently working on a novel and book of lyric essays.

DONNA HILL

DONNA HILL began her career in 1987 writing short stories for the confession magazines. Since that time she has more than 70 published titles to her credit since her first novel was released in 1990, and is considered one of the early pioneers of the African American romance genre. Three of her novels have been adapted for television. She has been featured in *Essence*, the New York *Daily News, USA Today, Today's Black Woman*, and *Black Enterprise* among many others. She has received numerous awards for her body of work—which crosses several genres—including The Career Achievement Award, the first recipient of The Trailblazer Award, The Zora Neale Hurston Literary Award, The Gold Pen Award among others, as well as commendations for her community service. As an editor she has packaged several highly successful novels, and anthologies, two of which were nominated for awards. Donna has been a writing instructor with the Elders Writing Program sponsored by Medgar Evers College through Poets & Writers. Donna is a graduate of Goddard College with an MFA in Creative Writing and is currently in pursuit of her Ph.D. in Secondary & Adult Education. She is an Adjunct Professor of English at Essex County College, Baruch College, and Medgar Evers College. Her other works for Spider Road Press are the poem "Horizons" included in the anthology *In The Questions: Poetry by and About Strong Women*, and the flash fiction piece "Super Mom" in the collection *Up Do*. Donna's most recent mystery novel is *Murder In The Aisles*. Donna lives in Brooklyn, NY, with her family.

JENNIFER LEEPER

JENNIFER LEEPER is an award-winning fiction author. Ms. Leeper's fiction includes *Padre*, a novella published by J. Burrage Publications. Ms. Leeper has also had short works of fiction published in *Independent Ink Magazine, Notes Magazine and The Stone Hobo*. Additionally, Ms. Leeper's short work of fiction noir, *Murder Brokers*, was published in a compilation, entitled *Fiction Noir: Thirteen Stories*, published by Hen House Press. In 2012, Ms. Leeper was awarded the Catoctin Mountain Artist-in-Residency, and in 2013, Ms. Leeper was a Tuscany Prize Novella Award finalist through Tuscany Press for her short novel, *Tribe*. Ms. Leeper's short story "Tatau," was published by Alternating Current Press in the journal, *Poiesis,* and was shortlisted as a finalist for the Luminaire Award in 2015. *Padre: The Narrowing Path* was published by Barking Rain Press in the summer of 2014. Ms. Leeper's short story, "The Gospel of Chloride," won a 2015 Tuscany Short Story Award honorable mention through Tuscany Press. In 2015, Whispering Prairie Press published Ms. Leeper's short story Ascent in Kansas City Voices and Every Day Fiction published The Bench, a flash fiction piece. Barking Rain Press will release *Border Run and Other Stories* in 2016.

PATRICIA FLAHERTY PAGAN

PATRICIA FLAHERTY PAGAN, Editor loves writing and reading about complex female characters. She is the author of *Trail Ways Pilgrims: Stories* and the writer of award-winning literary and crime short stories such as "Bargaining" and "Blood-red Geraniums." She edited *Up, Do: Flash Fiction by Women Writers*. Her short story about murder & molasses, "Bitter Sweets," was featured in *Eve's Requiem*. Her poem about Emma and Lizzie Borden, "Proposal After An Acquittal" was recently published in *Hair Raising Tales of Horror*. She teaches flash fiction writing at Writespace in Houston. After earning her MFA from the intensive writing program at Goddard College, she founded Spider Road Press to champion writing by and/or about strong women. An adoptive mom, she spends her free time composing silly poems with her son. Learn more about her and her upcoming events on her website: www.patriciaflahertypagan.com. Follow her on Twitter @PFwriteright.

MEGAN STEUSLOFF

Emerging writer MEGAN STEUSLOFF is an elementary school reading specialist and freelance writer from southeastern Michigan. She is a proud graduate of Oakland University, and a self-declared lifelong learner. She is fascinated by history and has big dreams for the future. Megan is happily married and has two beautiful children that keep her very busy and joyfully blessed. She loves going on adventures of all sizes with her family, reading, writing, gardening, taking long walks, and traveling. Megan strives to play, listen, explore, imagine, create, and laugh every day with her wonderful students and her own amazing kids. Megan has been published in numerous magazines, including *Authenticity for Women, Stone Voices, War Cry*, and *Valley Living*, and is a contributing author in the *It's Really 10 Months: Special Delivery* anthology. Visit Megan's blog at <u>megansteusloff.wordpress.com</u> and her website at <u>megansteusloff.weebly.com</u>.

FLASH FICTION CONTRIBUTORS

MELISSA (MEL) ALGOOD is a proud Navy Brat who's moved twelve times in her life. She earns a living as a hairstylist and resides with her boyfriend and their tuxedo cat Madame Bijou just outside of Houston, Texas. She loves to binge watch T.V., listen to music, eat Mexican food, and read Kafka. Her debut novel *Blood On The Potomac* was published by Inklings earlier this year. Mel's horror story "Hair Dying" was a finalist in The 2015 Channillo Short Story Contest. She co-edited *Hair Raising Tales of Horror*, which will be published by Limitless Ink in fall 2016. She's addicted to Twitter, so follow her @melalgood, and her blog http://melalgoodauthor.com where you can read her work.

HELEN ANGOVE began her working life as an electrical engineer on the south coast of England, and then worked briefly as a pricing analyst. She trained to be a priest in the Church of England, and spent seven years in full time ministry. These days, she lives with her husband and two children in Southern California. She wrote a long-running series of monthly articles for the British website Surefish, on the experiences of a British expatriate living in the United States, and three short stories—two published in science fiction anthologies, and one in an anthology of paranormal murder mysteries. She has written three novels, and am currently working on a fourth.

Award-winning novelist and poet ANDREA BARBOSA is an avid reader, soccer fanatic and a tourist at heart. She took Creative Writing classes at Texas Tech University and was a contributor writer for Yahoo Contributor Network. Her poetry collection *Holes in Space* is the recipient of the 2015 Silver Medal Award in Poetry from Readers' Favorite, and is featured in the 50 Best Books of 2014 at ReadFree.ly website, voted top 5 in poetry by readers. She currently serves as Author Events Director for the Houston Writers Guild. For more of her writing, follow her blog: http://massiveblackholenovel.blogspot.com/ Follow her on twitter at: @andyb0810

KATHRYN KULPA is the author of the flash fiction collection *Girls on Film,* which was published in 2016 by Paper Nautilus, and *Who's the Skirt?,* a micro-chapbook published by the Origami Poems Project. She received the Mid-List Press First Series Award for her short story collection *Pleasant Drugs* (Mid-List Press). Kathryn has published short fiction in *Bellevue Literary Review, Cleaver, decomP, Florida Review, Hayden's Ferry Review, Literary Orphans, Metazen, Monkeybicycle, NANO Fiction, Superstition Review,* and *Up, Do,* among others. She is the flash fiction editor at Cleaver and formerly served as an editor of Newport Review.

EDEN ROYCE has had over a dozen short stories published in various anthologies, including *Up, Do.* Her collection, *Spook Lights: Southern Gothic Horror* is on the Horror Writer's Association's recommended reading list. Eden is one of the writers for *The 7 Magpies* project, a first of its kind: a short horror film anthology written and directed entirely by black women. She is also the horror submissions editor for Mocha Memoirs Press where she conceived and edited several anthologies, one of which is *The Grotesquerie,* twenty-one horror short stories written by women.

KATE SPITZMILLER is a former ancient history teacher and currently works as a history tutor for a women's hockey team. She lives in Littleton, Massachusetts with three dogs, three cats and lots of books. Her short story "Poppy" was published in the *New England Writers Network Journal* in 1999. Her historical fiction novel *Andromache* will be published by Spider Road Press in late 2017.

HOLLY WALRATH is a writer, editor, poet, and the Associate Director of Writespace, a nonprofit literary center in Houston, Texas. She attended the University of Texas at Austin for her B.A. in English and the University of Denver for her M.L.A in Creative Writing. She has spoken at Houston YA/MG, Houston SCBWI, and internationally at the Child and the Book Conference. Her writing has appeared or is forthcoming in *Pulp Literature, The Vestal Review, and Spider Road Press,* among others. Holly currently resides in Seabrook, Texas.

ACKNOWLEDGMENTS

In addition to our generous donors, I would like to thank Alex, my most important "creative endeavor," Steve, for encouragement and taking on extra diaper duty, Kessika Johnson, David Welling, Violet Moore, and cover designer Heidi Dorey for their skilled work. Thanks to Gay Yellen, Sakhile Ross and our other beta readers, as well as Skipjack Publishing, Kate Spitzmiller, Carla Conrad, Mel Algood, my sisters Karen and MaryEllen, Inna Vyadro, Jody T. Morse, and Donna Hill for all their sound advice and support.

Thank you for supporting Spider Road Press!
If you enjoyed this collection, you will also enjoy:

Up, Do: Flash Fiction by Women Writers

Discover thirty-three literary & science fiction short, short stories by award winning and emerging female writers! Enjoy brief yet surprisingly rich slices of life for busy readers. This anthology is available from our website at www.spiderroadpress.com, on Amazon, and in select indie bookstores.

Trail Ways Pilgrims: Stories by Patricia Flaherty Pagan

How far would you go to become a mother? To find love? To leave your loss behind? Experience five haunting short stories from Patricia Flaherty Pagan, the award-winning writer of "Pillion 2006" and "Blood-Red Geraniums." E-book available on Amazon.com and Smashwords. Limited edition paperback available soon on our website.

Eve's Requiem: Tales of Women, Mystery, and Horror

Enjoy thirteen stories of peril and survival while sipping tea on a dark night. Featuring new horror, dark mystery, and crime stories from celebrated writers. This anthology is available from our website at www.spiderroadpress.com, on Amazon, and in select indie bookstores.

In the Questions: Poetry by and about Strong Women

Living in the questions is liberating, challenging, surprising, and at turns, painful and beautiful. Explore these poems and step into the questions with us. This anthology is available from our website and on Amazon.com.

Spider Road Press
Houston, TX
www.spiderroadpress.com

Made in the USA
San Bernardino, CA
19 February 2017